FIELD OF DEATH

FIELD OF DEATH

Stephen Overholser

GUNSMOKE

This hardback edition 2009
by BBC Audiobooks Ltd
by arrangement with
Golden West Literary Agency

ISBN 978 1 405 68257 2

British Library Cataloguing in Publication Data available.

Printed and bound in Great Britain by
CPI Antony Rowe, Chippenham and Eastbourne

Chapter I

Young Aaron Mills fell in love with Sadie Anne the first time he saw her. In later years Aaron came to realize that love-struck August afternoon of his six-teenth year marked the end of his boyhood and the beginning of his manhood.

That day Aaron escorted his mother and older sister, Jennifer, to the outsized front door of the Armbrister mansion, then he walked the length of the portico in search of shade and a cool breeze. He found no relief from summer's dog days, but in looking out to the horizon he did have a grand view of the flat, sun-cooked Colorado prairie. Turning and walking to the other end of the portico, Aaron looked due west and saw snow and glaciers on the distant peaks of the Rocky Mountains. He had never been in those mountains.

For a moment Aaron wished he was there in what he imagined was carefree coolness; the next mo-ment Aaron wanted to be nowhere else but here.

The great door of the mansion eased open several inches. The movement caught Aaron's eye. He saw a young woman slip out through the aperture. She was tall. Her waist was very small and her breasts very full. Long auburn hair fell around her face in soft curls, framing red lips and brown, doe eyes. She walked gracefully to Aaron. Her lips parted sensually as she spoke, and Aaron was caught in her spell.

"I don't like your sister," she said.

Aaron grinned. Throughout the summer his expression had been glum as he dutifully escorted his mother and sister around Denver and performed all of the gentlemanly tasks that were expected of him. For the past two years—going on three and forever, he feared—Aaron's role as the "perfect young gentleman" was defined entirely by his mother. Aaron's father had recently expanded his printing business and now spent little time at home.

Aaron stoically went through all of the correct motions. As needed, he held an umbrella or parasol over coiffured heads. He helped his mother and sister in and out of the new family carriage. And he opened and closed countless doors for the Mills women.

Because the Mills women never ventured far from the safe, settled sections of Denver, Aaron's travels were limited and his only adventures were those that he fantasied. In 1891 the streets around Capitol Hill and Armbrister Hill were paved with brick, the homes along the tree-lined streets were uniformly tidy, and the men and women on the walks were generally civilized and proper.

By contrast, many of the sprawling city's streets were only muddy or dusty tracks between long rows of dreary frame buildings. The boardwalks in the saloon district near the railyards were crowded with rowdy men and painted ladies. Of the men, some were cowboys and ranchers who had come into Denver after the sale of their stock. Others were miners and mill workers from the mountains. These were a rough breed, of various nationalities—Italians,

Frenchmen, Germans, Poles, Spaniards, Cornishmen, Russians—who stormed into Denver to let off steam and see the elephant.

Aaron's regular pastime at age sixteen was to read the crime news in the Denver newspapers. He was fascinated by the goings-on in the city's rougher sections, but he was shielded from seeing them for himself by his mother. The nearest Aaron came to being in Denver's saloon district was an occasional carriage ride across town to the new Mills Job Printers building. Aaron's time, for the most part, was carefully divided between the Hawkins Academy for Boys, where Aaron attended school, and the Mills home at the base of Armbrister Hill.

Armbrister Hill was the peak of Denver's high society. The pine-studded hill was topped by the famous Armbrister mansion. This grand structure was embraced by a tall iron fence in the shape of hundreds of upturned spears, and was guarded at the front gate by a pair of stone lions. Half fortress and half luxurious residence was the outside appearance of the mansion. Two high turrets stood at either end. The building between them was built of Colorado granite, trimmed with Colorado marble, and all of the interior metalwork was plated with Colorado gold.

Wallace Armbrister, builder of the mansion, was known in his lifetime as the Gold Baron of Colorado. He was one of thousands of young men who flocked to the Rockies in the rush of '59. But unlike the multitudes, Wallace Armbrister stumbled onto a bonanza. With his fortune, he built a flamboyant reputation and the greatest mansion Denver would ever see. And then at the zenith of his life, Wallace Armbrister shot himself through the brain in a Denver hotel room. This event took place in 1875, the year of Aaron's birth.

Wallace Armbrister's widow, Harriet, inherited the fortune and the mansion, but she became financially stingy and socially gracious in order to live down her late husband's reputation as a reckless philanthropist and a man for the ladies. Harriet, though plain, was known as "The Queen of the Queen City," but on that hot August afternoon when she greeted the Mills women at her front door, Aaron saw her for what she was: a bent, shriveled woman now well into her seventies, white-haired and drawn about the face as though she were in constant pain.

Perhaps she was. Less than a decade after her husband's suicide she suffered through a second tragedy when her only child, a daughter named Cleo, was thrown from her horse during a Fourth of July parade. Cleo was trampled to death by a following team of draft horses that pulled a red, white, and blue ore wagon. The big wagon was loaded with gold ore from the Colorado Rockies.

Cleo Armbrister had endured a life of endless wealth and unkind remarks. She had inherited her mother's looks and a streak of madness from her father. Cleo believed she was a great horsewoman and set out to prove it by riding half wild horses in the city's parades. These animals pranced, pitched, ran sideways for great distances, and were inclined to bite any human in sight.

Some of the jokes about Cleo found their way into print in the less reputable newspapers of the day. One reporter claimed to have seen a man observe Cleo Armbrister in a parade and wonder aloud which was the horse. Disparaging remarks followed

Cleo to her grave. A story made the rounds that although Denver's "Princess of the Prairie" had been trampled by horses, no one could tell the difference. And in truth, despite the riches her name represented, Cleo was probably well on her way to spinsterhood when she was killed at the age of twenty-four.

Harriet Armbrister left Denver immediately after her daughter's funeral. The servants were let go. The mansion gate was bolted. Huge stained glass windows at ground level were boarded over.

No one in Denver knew where Harriet had gone. Rumors sprung up. Harriet Armbrister had booked passage on a steamship bound for the Continent, but she had leaped overboard in mid-ocean. Another rumor had it that Harriet now lived quietly back East, refusing to speak to anyone. Her sadness was so profound that she would never return to the West. Broken hearts do not mend.

Everyone in Denver wondered what would happen to the grandest residence in the city, the Armbrister mansion. Weeds grew up in the drive and spread to the lawn. Trimmed shrubs grew raggedly. Passersby peered through the gate and shook their heads at the forlorn sight of the proud mansion with its boarded windows and chained front door. Within the year the mansion was said to be haunted by the ghosts of a mad Wallace Armbrister and his hideous daughter, Cleo.

But in two years Harriet returned. She brought a teenaged girl and made it known that she had adopted the girl. And when Harriet presented her to Denver society in a debutante ball the likes of which Denverites had never seen before, everyone realized the girl possessed all that Cleo had lacked. This young woman was a beauty in the classic mold, with a perfect hourglass figure, and an angelic face. So great was her feminine power that she could stop a man in his tracks or bring a bud to flower with a mere glance. Such was the talk.

One fact came to light, however, that brought a hush. Harriet Armbrister called her adopted daughter by the name of Cleo.

Aaron was vaguely aware of these circumstances, and of the many rumors that had heated cold parlors last winter, but in his sixteenth year he was much more interested in crime news and the lurid accounts of murder and mayhem he read in the *Police Gazette*. Aaron had also recently discovered dime novels. He had an active imagination. As he read, he virtually lived the lives of famous explorers, hunters, Indians, and soldiers, and he rode the Owlhoot Trail with courageous lawmen in their relentless pursuit of outlaws.

Aaron's interest in these garish publications intensified when his mother, after being tipped off by Jennifer, confiscated his entire collection. Thereafter, Aaron, who always had to buy the dime novels through his friends at school, sneaked them into the house beneath his shirt. He hid them under the bottom drawer of a clothes chest in his bedroom. Reading the forbidden stories in secret made them more exciting than ever.

"I don't like your sister."

Aaron realized he was smiling crazily, but could not stop himself. "What . . . what did she do to you?"

"She dismissed me. I live there, but she dismissed me. Can you imagine?"

Aaron nodded. "Jennifer does that when she's through talking to someone who's younger than she."

The young woman glanced back toward the door. "Your sister calls you 'that young man.'"

"You should hear what I call her," Aaron said recklessly.

The young woman laughed suddenly. "I'd like to, Aaron."

Aaron felt a blush sweep over his face when she spoke his name. "What's your name?" he asked.

The young woman reached out and took Aaron's hand. She twisted his arm, hard. Aaron's obvious confusion brought another laugh from the girl.

"Can't you guess?" she asked.

Aaron shook his head. "Who are you? Do you work here?"

"Armtwister," she said. "My name is Armtwister."

Suddenly Aaron realized she was the legendary girl, the adopted daughter of Harriet Armbrister. "You are . . . Cleo."

Her face darkened. "I am not. My name is Moose. Moose Armtwister."

Aaron laughed. "Wait until old Harriet hears about this." He made an elaborate pretense of calling out, "Mrs. Armbrister!"

"Don't," the young woman whispered urgently. She moved closer and touched Aaron with the length of her body. The pleasant sensation made Aaron feel excited and uncomfortable at once.

"I hate that name," she whispered. "Please don't call me that."

"What do you want to be called?" Aaron asked. "Besides Moose."

A smile crept over her face. "I like you."

Aaron swallowed hard and tried to think of something to say, but failed. All he could do was grin.

"Sadie Anne," she said. "Call me Sadie Anne."

"That's a pretty name," Aaron said.

She nodded seriously. "It was my mother's."

"Where are you from?" Aaron asked.

"Not far from here," she said. She stepped away from Aaron, but held on to his hand. Aaron followed her eyes as she looked out across the portico to the prairie out east.

"Out there?" Aaron asked.

The question was never answered. The door of the mansion swung open. Aaron's mother and sister came outside, followed by Harriet Armbrister. Mrs. Armbrister made a quick, beckoning motion to her adopted daughter.

Aaron whispered, "Good-by, Sadie Anne."

"Don't say good-by—ever," Sadie Anne whispered, then turned and walked across the portico to Mrs. Armbrister's side.

Aaron caught up with his mother and sister before they reached the carriage. High in the driver's seat, the hired man took reins in hand and held the team. Aaron opened the carriage door and helped his mother and sister in, then he climbed in after them.

Aaron looked back at Sadie Anne and Mrs. Armbrister. Sadie Anne raised her hand in what might have been a secret wave. The carriage moved ahead.

Jennifer glanced at her mother, then spoke to Aaron. "Well, you two seemed to get along very well."

Aaron shrugged in reply.

Jennifer went on in a teasing voice, "I'll bet you're the only young man in town to have held that young lady's hand. Harriet never lets her out of the house, they say."

The carriage rolled through the gate, past the stone lions, and entered the street. Aaron wanted to look back to see if Sadie Anne was still there, but he forced himself to watch the passing scenery.

Aaron's mother said, "I certainly would wonder about the girl's background. All kinds of children end up in those orphanages back in New England."

"Where?" Aaron asked.

"Pay attention, Aaron," Jennifer said.

Aaron's mother explained, "Harriet said she had adopted the girl over a year ago from an orphanage in Boston. Did she say anything about her background to you?"

Aaron shook his head.

"The way you two were holding hands," Jennifer said, "I just wonder what you were talking about."

"Well, she is pretty," Aaron's mother said. "But her manners are rusty."

"Nonexistent," Jennifer said. "She is no Cleo."

"Isn't it odd that Harriet insists on calling her by that name," Aaron's mother said.

"Harriet's living in a dream world," Jennifer said. "She simply can't face the fact that she's lost her daughter."

"Perhaps so," Mrs. Mills said slowly. She looked at Jennifer. "I can understand that."

The carriage descended the slope to the base of Armbrister Hill. Around the corner at the first street, Maple Avenue, the Mills home stood among other brick and frame houses. Most were two story, and most were painted in reds and whites, sporting gingerbread decorations and latticework.

Aaron looked out of the carriage window at the familiar neighborhood scene, but he saw none of it. Sadie Anne's voice still echoed in his mind and he saw a lingering vision of her.

Chapter II

In the following days Aaron overheard his mother and sister repeat their severe judgments of Sadie Anne to their friends. Aaron wanted to defend Sadie Anne, but he kept silent. He knew he would only start an argument with his mother. Aaron had learned from past experience that it was easier to go around his mother than through her.

Aaron began taking evening walks in the neighborhood while his mother and Jennifer sat at home reading aloud to one another, sewing, or painting china. Aaron's father, Jacob Mills, was swamped with orders for printing and was rarely home before eight o'clock.

Aaron's walks, by design, took him up Armbrister Hill. He walked slowly past the great mansion, hoping to see Sadie Anne "by accident." Aaron planned elaborate explanations for his presence in front of the mansion, and he imagined himself smoothly engaging Sadie Anne in witty conversation. Aaron also wanted to find out what Sadie Anne had meant when she'd said she did not live far away. Certainly she had not meant Boston, Massachusetts.

After several days Aaron realized his plan would never work. The street was too far from the mansion, and Aaron did not yet have the courage to walk through the gate.

Next Aaron hiked up the weed-grown hillside behind his house. He climbed to the thick stand of pine trees near the top of Armbrister Hill. He walked through the fragrant trees to the iron fence that surrounded the Armbrister property. From here the mansion was even farther away than it was from the street, over a hundred yards distant. A summerhouse stood halfway between the fence and the mansion. The small building was octagonal with a peaked roof and screened sides.

Aaron noticed several places along the fence where he could crawl under, and he was tempted to sneak in for a closer look. But the prospect of getting caught was more frightening than walking through the front gate.

The next evening Aaron did that. He walked past the stone lions, up the walk, and mounted the steps to the portico. At the mansion's front door, Aaron turned the bell handle. His knees quivered while he waited, and he desperately hoped Sadie Anne would open the front door.

After a few long minutes the door was opened by a uniformed maid. "Sir?" she asked.

"I've come to call on Miss Armbrister," Aaron said.

"Who shall I say is calling?" The young maid spoke in an Irish brogue.

"Aaron Mills."

The maid smiled briefly, then closed the door. Aaron endured another long wait. The more time that passed, the higher his expectations rose. Earlier, Aaron had planned exactly what he would say to Sadie Anne, but now his mind was blank.

Finally the door was again opened by the Irish maid. But instead of admitting Aaron, she stood in the doorway and spoke without looking up at his face.

"Miss Armbrister is not at home, sir."

"When is she expected?" Aaron asked.

"I don't know, sir." Still the maid's eyes were downcast.

Aaron paused. "All right. I'll come back tomorrow."

The maid looked up and for a moment she seemed ready to speak openly, but in the next moment she backed into the entryway and closed the door.

Aaron was puzzled. He sensed the maid's shame, but did not understand it.

At home that evening Mrs. Mills asked Aaron what he was doing on these evening walks of his. Aaron said he was exercising so he would be in condition for the Hawkins Academy fencing team in the fall. Even though Aaron did plan to try out for the fencing team next school year, he turned away from his mother and climbed the stairs to his bedroom, knowing that was the first outright lie he had ever told her.

That night Aaron lay awake in his darkened room. His thoughts were jumbled and upsetting. He wondered about Sadie Anne. Deep down he had a fear that he would never see her again. As he tried to push that fear away, he began to regret the lie he had told his mother. What if she found out he had gone to the Armbrister mansion? Then Aaron heard his father come into the house. The front door closed. Muffled voices came from the main hall. Presently Aaron heard his father's deliberate footfalls as he came up the staircase and walked to the end of the hall, followed by the lighter footsteps of Mrs. Mills. Aaron drifted off to sleep, realizing he had not seen his father face to face in a long time. One week . . . two weeks . . . Aaron could not remember how long.

The next evening Aaron returned to the Armbrister mansion. The Irish maid answered the door.

"Well, here I am," Aaron said.

The maid again avoided his eyes. "I'm sorry, sir, but Miss Armbrister is out for the evening."

All day Aaron had planned for this moment. "When will she be back?"

"I don't know, sir."

"Look at me," Aaron said.

The maid shook her head.

"I know you're lying," Aaron said. "She's here, isn't she?"

The maid did not reply. She stood in the doorway with her head bowed. Aaron felt a sudden urge to shove past her and rush into the mansion. He pictured himself running through endless, golden hallways, searching and calling out for Sadie Anne.

"Why are you lying?" Aaron demanded. Then he realized the maid was crying. He had not foreseen this. "I'm sorry," he said. "I didn't mean to shout at you."

The Irish maid brushed her cheeks with the back of her hand. Aaron realized she was little older than he was. He regretted bullying her and watched in silence as she backed into the entryway and closed the door.

Aaron walked home, feeling angry and frustrated. He was certain the maid was lying, and he was equally certain Mrs. Harriet Armbrister was behind the lie. At home Aaron went straight to his bedroom and tried to plan a way to get past Mrs. Armbrister. He had no success. The mansion was a fortress, and Mrs. Armbrister was queen of the realm.

Aaron believed he could not sleep, but at last he did. His angry thoughts became dreams. Sadie Anne was bound in chains. She was held prisoner by a white-haired witch. Aaron tried to rescue her, but failed.

Early in the morning Aaron awoke, troubled by vague memories of nightmares. But he awoke with a new idea. He would confront Mrs. Armbrister. Aaron grew impatient as the hot day wore on, and in the middle of the afternoon he left the house without telling his mother where he was going. He climbed the hill to the Armbrister mansion and rang the bell at the front door.

"Oh, no," the Irish maid whispered when she opened the door.

"Yes, it's me," Aaron said. "Tell Mrs. Harriet Armbrister that I want to speak to her."

The maid hesitated.

"I won't leave until I have," Aaron said.

The maid nodded and closed the door. Several minutes passed. When the door opened again, Aaron stood face to face with the queen of the realm.

"You've become something of a pest, young man," Mrs. Armbrister said. "I expected better from the Mills family."

"I didn't expect to be lied to every time I came to call on Sadie Anne," Aaron said. He immediately realized his error. "I mean, Cleo."

At the mention of Sadie Anne, Mrs. Armbrister flinched. Her face reddened. "You're impudent."

"Why won't you allow me to see her?" Aaron asked.

"Young man, whatever makes you imagine my daughter *wants* to see you?" Mrs. Armbrister demanded.

For a moment Aaron was stopped. Had he misjudged Sadie Anne? He said haltingly, "Well, if she doesn't want to see me, she can tell me herself, can't she?"

"Oh, never mind," Mrs. Armbrister said, dismissing the whole conversation with a wave of her bony hand. "I'm looking out for my daughter's best interests. That's all you need to know. Good day." She stepped back and started to close the door.

Aaron placed his hand on the door and held it open. "Mrs. Armbrister, I won't leave until I've spoken to Sadie . . . to her."

"Nonsense," Mrs. Armbrister said. "I'll simply send word to your mother to come and get you. I daresay she'll be displeased."

Aaron did not want to be intimidated by the old woman, but he realized he would get nowhere this way. He blurted, "You can't hold Sadie Anne prisoner!" As soon as he spoke, Aaron felt overcome by an odd sensation. Last night he had shouted the same words in his dream. For a moment he relived the dream as he looked at the white-haired witch.

"Don't call her by that name!" Mrs. Armbrister shouted. She took a deep, labored breath. "Young man, you appear to have the wrong idea. I'm providing guidance for the girl. She's not had an easy life. Cleo does not need to be bothered by a young man now." Mrs. Armbrister added, "Someday she'll thank me."

Aaron said, "Someday she'll hate you."

"That's quite enough!" Mrs. Armbrister said angrily.

"I suggest you leave. I won't send word to your mother. I'll send word to the city marshal and have you removed from my land."

Aaron stared at Mrs. Armbrister for a long moment before turning away. He deliberately walked slowly down the steps and along the walk, but when he reached the drive, his anger and frustration overtook him. He slapped a fist into one hand and ran out to the street and down the hill. He was breathless and wet with sweat when he ran up Maple Avenue to his house, but he was still angry.

Aaron glumly ate supper with his mother and sister. Jennifer chatted with her mother about an upcoming social event. Aaron paid less attention than usual. Once, when Mrs. Mills spoke to him, she had to repeat her question to get through to Aaron.

After the meal Aaron left the table and went upstairs to his room. Half an hour later his mother called out from the foot of the stairs.

"Aaron, someone is here to see you."

Aaron went downstairs, half fearing he would find the city marshal there. In the front hallway Aaron saw his mother standing beside the Irish maid from the Armbrister mansion.

"This young lady wishes to speak to you, Aaron."

The maid stared pleadingly at Aaron, but said nothing.

"Mother, may we be alone?" Aaron asked.

"Oh . . . of course," Mrs. Mills said stiffly. She walked down the hall to the kitchen. Jennifer stood in the doorway there. Mrs. Mills closed the door.

"I'm sorry I lied to you," the maid said to Aaron. "Mrs. Armbrister made me."

"I know," Aaron said. "I don't hold it against you."

"God will," she said with a pained expression on her face. "I've sinned." She nearly broke into tears. After a moment she went on, "I lied because Mrs. Armbrister told me to. I was afraid of losing my job."

"I understand," Aaron said.

"I should not have listened to Mrs. Armbrister," the maid said. "I should not have sinned. I've quit. I'll never go back there." She retreated toward the door. "I'm on my way to church now, to confess."

The maid opened the door, then reached into her handbag and brought out an envelope. "Miss Armbrister—your Sadie Anne—asked me to give you this."

Aaron took the envelope.

"I must go," the maid said, stepping out to the porch. "Good-by."

"Thank you," Aaron said, holding up the envelope. "Good luck."

Aaron pulled the door shut and turned around. His mother and Jennifer came out of the kitchen. From the look of happy anticipation on Jennifer's face, Aaron knew his mother was angered at him.

"What was that all about?' Mrs. Mills asked. Jennifer hovered behind her.

"Nothing," Aaron said. "Nothing important."

Mrs. Mills glanced at the envelope Aaron held. "Who was that girl?"

Aaron did not reply. In the long, uncomfortable moment that passed, he made a decision. He would defy his mother. He would refuse to answer her questions.

Behind Aaron, the door opened. Jacob Mills came in. Jennifer squealed with delight and rushed to her father and hugged him. The moment of tension was broken. Aaron turned and looked at his father. Aaron was surprised to see how tired he looked. Jacob Mills was a big man, but in recent years he had grown barrel-bellied, and now his bulk seemed to pull him down like an anchor.

"I had hoped to get home in time for supper," Jacob Mills said, smiling tiredly. "But I see I'm late again."

"Your supper's in the warmer," Mrs. Mills said. "Come, and I'll serve it to you."

Jacob Mills walked down the hall toward the dining room, giving Aaron a cheerful but soft slap across the shoulder as he passed by. Mrs. Mills followed her husband and daughter, but she glanced back at Aaron. *I will speak to you later,* her expression said.

Aaron climbed the stairs to his room. After closing the door, he tore open the envelope and read the note Sadie Anne had penned on perfumed stationery.

Dearest Aaron,

I did not know you had tried to visit me until Eileen told me yesterday that Mother had ordered her to lie to you. I am so sorry you were turned away. I did want to see you. I hope you believe me when I say that I had nothing to do with the lies you were told.

I am sad to have to tell you that I am going away. In the morning Mother and I leave on the train for New York City where I will attend a finishing school.

I do not know if I will return to Denver next summer. I hope to, if only to see you. I'll never forget you, Aaron. Please do not forget me.

Love,
Sadie Anne

Aaron's throat drew tight and ached. He was close to tears, but did not let them come. Presently he heard his mother mount the stairs. Her footfalls stopped outside his door.

"Aaron."

Chapter III

Aaron let his mother into the bedroom. She closed the door and turned around and faced him.

"Aaron, I don't know what's gotten into you, but I don't like it, I can tell you that. Now, who was that young lady? Tell me what that was all about."

Under his mother's stare, Aaron lost some of his resolve to defy his mother. "She brought a note from Sadie Anne."

"Sadie Anne?" Mrs. Mills asked.

"Mrs. Armbrister's daughter," Aaron said. He added, "Adopted daughter."

"Oh, you mean Cleo," Mrs. Mills said. "Have you been seeing her on these mysterious evening walks you've been taking?"

Aaron shook his head.

"But the girl writes notes to you," Mrs. Mills said. "Bold, isn't she? Aaron, I honestly don't think you should be interested in her. Oh, she's lovely, of course. I can understand how your head could be turned by her. But she acts like a tart."

Aaron felt a rush of anger and nearly shouted at his mother. "Don't talk that way about her!" He paused, seeing he had surprised his mother, then said, "Sadie Anne is going to school back East."

"I see," Mrs. Mills said. She looked down at the sheet of stationery Aaron held. "That explains the note.

Well, I'm sure that is best for all concerned." She turned away and left the bedroom.

Aaron closed the door and went to his desk. He tried to write a poem on the subject of lost love. His title was "The Worst For All Concerned." Aaron thought it was important that he put his thoughts into words, but after writing two lines, he found he could not concentrate. His thoughts were jumbled. He felt a deep sense of loss, of sadness, and he still harbored the fear that he would never again see Sadie Anne.

After a time Aaron gave up on the poem. None of the words he wrote took full measure of the depth of his feelings. He tore the paper into small pieces, then reread the note Sadie Anne had sent. He put the note into its envelope and hid it beneath the bottom drawer of his dresser along with his collection of dime novels and *Police Gazettes*.

In September Aaron fell into step with the forty-three other boys who attended Hawkins Academy. Aaron did not long mope over lost love, but he did not forget Sadie Anne, either. Throughout the school year she lived in his most private thoughts, and in lonely moments Aaron tried to visualize her.

Bad news came in the spring. Harriet Armbrister wrote to friends saying she would not return to Colorado this summer. She was taking her daughter to the Continent for travel and further education.

Aaron did not take this news well. He was kicked off the Hawkins Academy fencing team for ungentlemanly and aggressive behavior. He was transferred to the boxing club. Aaron had grown big enough through the arms and shoulders to be a good boxer, but he lacked skill. The coach worked with him and tried to teach him the finer points of pugilism, but Aaron had little patience with the lessons.

He defeated his first opponent with sheer power. At home Aaron was sullen toward his mother and abusive to his sister.

Aaron's life took a new turn when school let out in June. His father put him to work in the shop as a printer's devil. The foreman at Mills Job Printers was a big, loud-voiced man named Charley Simms. He ruled the shop tyrannically. Aaron had met Charley Simms two or three times, and even though Jacob Mills had often told his family he owed much of the shop's success to his foreman, Aaron had never liked the man. Perhaps Aaron feared Simms's loud voice and gruff manner.

By her grim expression, Aaron knew that his mother did not approve of this summer employment. Aaron suspected she had agreed to let Aaron try it only because he had been in such a "mood" lately and was hard to handle at home.

Aaron learned the meaning of drudgery his first day on the job. At sunup he rode in the buggy with his father to the shop. Charley Simms was there, waiting. Jacob Mills formally introduced Aaron to the foreman, then went to his office in the front of the building.

Charley Simms was as big as Aaron remembered. His forearms were meaty, covered with dark, wiry hair, and his hands were platter-sized. Simms took Aaron around the shop and methodically explained the duties of a printer's devil. He showed Aaron the three big presses and pointed out their ink reservoirs that were to be kept filled at all times.

Along one wall were tall racks of type. After a run, Simms explained, all the used type had to be cleaned and replaced in the racks. He motioned across the width of the shop.

"Sweep the floor several times a day. Keep the scrap paper picked up. If any of my printers slip and fall because of a sheet of ink-covered paper on the floor, I'll have your hide. In the shop you ain't the boss's son. You're the printer's devil. Everybody's your boss. The sooner you get used to that idea, the better off you'll be."

Charley Simms spoke forcefully, but Aaron detected no meanness in the man. A job was to be done, and Simms expected Aaron to do it. Aaron saw this as a challenge and instead of dreading the summer's work, suddenly he was eager to prove himself.

Within the hour, when the four printers came to work and the presses started to run, so did Aaron. And Charley Simms came thundering behind him, bellowing commands faster than Aaron could possibly act on them.

All day Aaron raced from one job to another. He cleaned type and inky presses, but never to the big foreman's satisfaction.

"You call this clean?" Charley Simms demanded after he had inspected a rack of type Aaron had just cleaned. "Do it over again, devil. Hurry! Look over there! You've got a press to take care of!"

Aaron worked six days a week, ten hours a day. At night he was so stiff and sore that he could hardly sleep. When he did sleep, his dreams were filled with the voice of Charley Simms. Aaron no longer dreamed of Sadie Anne.

Every evening Mrs. Mills met her son at the back door of the house. Aaron usually took a trolley home, leaving his father working in the front office. Mrs. Mills scrubbed Aaron's hands and face, trying in vain to remove thick, black printer's ink. Aaron's skin became red and raw, but still the ink did not come out. By the end of the second week, she'd seen enough. When Jacob came home, she confronted him.

"Look, just look at his hands. Look at his face."

"How did he get so red?" Jacob Mills asked, grinning.

"Oh, Jacob!"

"Aaron's got ink in his blood," Jacob Mills said. "He'll make a good printer one day. Charley Simms says so."

Aaron had never received a compliment from Charley Simms and he was surprised and pleased that one had been given behind his back.

"Oh, Jacob, is that what you want?" Mrs. Mills asked. "Aaron's a young gentleman. He'll go to Denver College one day and enter a profession. You want that for your son, don't you?"

"Won't hurt him a bit to learn a trade," Jacob Mills said. "Every American boy should have a trade under his belt." He looked at Aaron. "You can still go on to college if you want to."

"Jacob—" Mrs. Mills stopped and spoke to Aaron. "Run upstairs to your room for a while, will you, dear?"

Aaron was too tired to run anywhere, but he left the dining room and went into the hallway. At the foot of the staircase, he turned back and listened.

"Jacob, you just don't understand, do you? If Aaron was tutored this summer, he would be far ahead of his classmates next year."

"Why should he be ahead of them?" Jacob Mills asked.

"You want Aaron to get ahead, don't you?"

"When he's grown, he'll have plenty of chances to

get ahead. Let the boy alone. Charley won't kill him."

"Aaron's wasting his time in that dirty shop. I never should have let you talk me into—"

Jacob Mills's voice rose when he interrupted her. "That *dirty shop* put that dress on you. That *dirty shop* built this house. That *dirty shop* bought you a fancy carriage and a man to drive it."

"Now, don't be angry—"

"My mind's made up," Jacob Mills said. "Aaron needs to be around men. Another summer with you and Jennifer, and he'd be sissified."

"Jacob!"

"It's true. You and Jennifer smother him."

"We do not! We've taught him to be a gentleman. You'll turn him into a savage."

"All I know is," Jacob Mills said, "that I should be teaching him the ways of men. I should spend more time with him, but I can't. There just ain't enough hours in a day." He added, "Don't fret over Aaron. Charley will be good for him."

"Charley Simms is a bully," Mrs. Mills said.

"No, he ain't," Jacob Mills said. "Charley may be hard, but he's a fair man."

Aaron heard Jennifer coming down the stairs. He quickly turned and went up a few steps before Jennifer saw him. They passed one another without speaking.

Before the month was out, Aaron learned that his father was right about Charley Simms. As Aaron became more proficient in his tasks, the foreman became less demanding. He no longer pursued Aaron.

Aaron developed a friendship with the printers. They had watched him carefully, Aaron was aware, until they saw that he worked hard and was not merely the boss's son who must be tolerated. The printers even began teasing Aaron.

Once a printer spoke to another as Aaron passed by. "That devil sure don't work hard."

The second printer, speaking louder than necessary, replied, "Near as I can figure, he spends most of his time sleeping out back in one of the trash bins."

"You reckon he's getting paid to do that?"

"Reckon so."

"That's an easy life."

"Sure is."

Aaron turned back and said to them, "If you two no-good printers would keep those presses running like you're supposed to, I'd be able to stay awake long enough to supervise you."

"Did you hear that?" the first printer asked the second.

He shook his head in disgust. "Sounded like a squeak in one of the presses to me."

The exchange took less than a minute, and the printers spoke over the sounds of the presses while they worked. Aaron walked away with a smile on his face. The real meaning of their teasing was that they accepted him and liked him.

Late in July Aaron began to learn the basics of the printer's trade. He learned to read type backwards, and he learned how to fill a printer's stick with type. Often Aaron would work faster at his regular jobs in order to gain some free time so he could be coached by one of the printers. Once Aaron caught Charley Simms watching as a printer showed him how to set type. Simms grinned before he turned and walked away.

The summer that began in misery ended in pleasure. Aaron's mother gave up trying to scrub him every night, even though she still grimaced when he came home in the evening.

The last day at work before school started, Charley Simms took Aaron off his job of cleaning a press and led him into Jacob Mills's office. Aaron felt strangely out of place here as he stood beside his father's great rolltop desk. Throughout the summer Aaron had rarely entered this office. He felt as though he belonged out in the shop with the "working men."

Jacob Mills's desk was heaped with papers—printed copy, order forms, correspondence. He turned in his swivel chair and smiled up at Aaron and Charley Simms.

"Gentlemen," he greeted them.

"Jake," Charley Simms said, "I'm here to tell you this boy of yours is one of the hardest workers I've ever seen. I hate to lose him. He's going to be hard to replace, mighty hard. If he wants to come back next summer, I'd recommend you hire him as an apprentice."

Aaron was surprised and stomach-quivering excited at once. He immediately pictured himself working in the shop as a printer. Although he did not know all there was to know about printing, Aaron was confident that he could learn. He was eager for the challenge.

Aaron saw that this moment was a proud one for his father, too. But even as Jacob Mills smiled, Aaron caught a frightening glimpse of the future. His father breathed raggedly through his mouth, and the weak smile soon faded. What Aaron sensed but could not have put into words was true. Jacob Mills would not live out the year.

Two weeks before Christmas of 1892, Charley Simms would discover his employer slumped over the rolltop desk, dead of heart failure. Early in the year of 1893 the family business would be sold to a competitor. Aaron's dream of working as a printer in his father's shop would never come true.

Chapter IV

Late in May of 1894 Aaron and forty-three class-mates graduated from the Hawkins Academy for Boys. Aaron's grades were average, but his performance in the boxing team had been outstanding. Aaron's style had become a mixture of a few lessons that had taken hold and his own aggressiveness and determination. Aaron had gone through his final year undefeated in the heavyweight class.

The evening following graduation ceremonies, Mrs. Mills told Aaron that she had arranged to hire tutors to guide his studies throughout the summer months. She said she wanted to be certain Aaron was well prepared for his freshman year at Denver College.

Aaron accepted these plans in silence. The death of Jacob Mills had hit his mother hard. She had visibly aged. Aaron wanted to offer comfort to her now, not arguments.

Aaron had been forced to give up his plans of working in the summer as a printer. Printing firms wanted permanent employees, not summer help. And the firm that had bought out Mills Job Printers had overextended and nearly gone broke. The presses and equipment had been auctioned off and now the Mills building stood empty.

On a snowy day last March Charley Simms had

come to the Mills home. He stood in the front hall-way, rather shyly, and kept his head bowed while he spoke. Melting snow glistened on his boots. He said that he had not been able to find work since Jake died. Now he was on his way to Cheyenne, Wyo-ming, where he had heard of a job in a small print shop. He planned to catch the morning northbound train.

Charley Simms held out his big right hand to Aaron. Aaron felt his strong grip as they shook hands.

"If I was married up," Charley Simms said, "and if I had a boy, I'd want him to be like you, Aaron. I know your father was mighty proud of you."

Emotion clogged Aaron's voice when he replied, "Thank you, Charley. I learned a lot from you."

Aaron did not voice his deepest thoughts. He wanted to tell Charley Simms not to go, as if his leaving somehow marked Aaron's final break with boyhood. Aaron sensed that his life was changing, but he did not know where the changes led.

Aaron watched Charley Simms pull on his sheep-skin hat, nod good-by to Mrs. Mills, turn and leave the house. The big man walked into the snowstorm and was swallowed by it.

Aaron saw many changes that winter. Jennifer no longer treated him like a savage who must be forced into the mold of a gentleman. When she was home, she spoke to him almost as an equal. But she was away from the house more often now. She was be-ing courted by a scarecrow of a law clerk named Oliver Hayes.

Throughout the month of June Aaron worked halfheartedly at his studies. He felt listless. Time floated by like summer clouds. In his free time Aaron took long walks in the neighborhood. Sometimes he ran to keep in shape. And sometimes he climbed Armbrister Hill.

Early in July Aaron became aware of increased activity at the Armbrister mansion. Men worked to clean the mansion's windows. Shrubs were caressed and trimmed and the grounds were tidied up. Bird droppings were scrubbed off the pair of lions at the gate.

On the fifth of July Aaron saw a freight wagon loaded with wooden boxes and steamer trunks lumber up the hill and turn in at the Armbrister mansion.

Aaron had been thinking of Sadie Anne ever since he had first noticed workmen around the mansion. He hoped she was coming back. He wondered if she had changed, if she felt the same way about him as she had when she wrote the note on perfumed stationery.

Three days later Aaron walked past the mansion. He heard someone running behind him.

"Aaron!"

Aaron turned and saw her. Sadie Anne ran to him, her long auburn hair trailing out like dark fire in the sunlight.

"Moose!" Aaron said.

Sadie Anne laughed and came to him, throwing her arms around him. She hugged him, then drew back.

"Aaron, look at you! You've sure filled out."

"You don't look so bad yourself, Sadie Anne," Aaron said.

"You remember my secret name," she said.

"I remember every word you ever said to me," Aaron said. "Or wrote to me."

"Oh, Aaron," Sadie Anne said softly. "I'm so sorry about what happened."

"That was a long time ago," Aaron said. "It wasn't your fault."

"Aaron," she whispered.

They looked at one another for a long moment, then Aaron took her in his arms. He kissed her, feeling her soft, warm lips with his own.

Sadie Anne kissed him back. Then she struggled away. "Aaron, not right here on the street!"

"Where, then?" he asked.

Sadie Anne laughed again. "You've changed in more ways than one."

Neither of them spoke. They held hands and looked into one another's eyes. Aaron had dreamed of this moment. The reality of it was far better.

Sadie Anne glanced back at the gate. "I have to go. We've only been here since last night. I happened to see you walk past, and I just ran after you. Why were you walking here?"

Aaron remembered the excuses he had once thought up. All of them seemed pointless now. "I was hoping to see you, Sadie Anne."

She smiled. "Aaron, come for a visit."

"How can I?" he said. "Mrs. Armbrister won't let me in the door."

"Oh, yes she will," Sadie Anne said. "I'll see to it. Can you come tomorrow evening about seven?"

"Yes," Aaron said, "if you're certain—"

"She'll listen to me," Sadie Anne said. "Come at seven." She turned and walked away. Aaron watched her until she passed through the gate between the stone lions.

After supper that night Aaron told his mother he intended to go to the Armbrister mansion the next evening and visit Sadie Anne.

"Who?" she asked.

"Mrs. Armbrister's adopted daughter," Aaron said.

"Oh . . . her," Mrs. Mills said. She looked thoughtful. "I didn't know Harriet was back in town." She added, "I don't get around as much as I once did."

Aaron looked at his mother, wondering if she even remembered Sadie Anne.

"Well," Mrs. Mills said with a sigh, "I suppose you're old enough to look out for yourself now. Just don't let that girl interfere with your studies."

Aaron said he wouldn't. He was surprised at his mother's mild reaction. She had changed. Their relationship had changed. Aaron wondered if Sadie Anne and Mrs. Armbrister had changed in their relationship, too.

At seven o'clock the following evening Aaron was met at the mansion's door by a stocky, dour-looking maid. She admitted Aaron and led him down a long hallway. She gestured to an arched doorway, then went on down the hall.

The arched doorway opened into a cavernous drawing room. Aaron felt as though he had shrunk as he walked into the room. The walls were lined with huge paintings. Some were landscapes and seascapes; others were portraits of men, larger than life-sized.

In the center of this room, appearing smaller than life-sized, were Mrs. Armbrister and Sadie Anne. They sat together on an upholstered settee. Aaron crossed the room to the two women, greeted them, and sat in an armchair that faced them.

Mrs. Armbrister looked even more frail than Aaron remembered her. Sitting beside Sadie Anne made the old woman look deathly. Aaron made appropriate small talk and received small answers to his questions from Mrs. Armbrister. After a few minutes the three sat in an atmosphere of strained silence.

Aaron was surprised by Sadie Anne's silence. He had expected her to be talkative and bold, perhaps even flippant. But she sat very still, ankles crossed, and her slender hands were folded in her lap. She avoided looking at Aaron, except for occasional glances.

Presently Mrs. Armbrister edged forward in the settee. She grimaced as she stood. Aaron heard the old woman excuse herself. She had nearly left the room before Aaron remembered his manners. He leaped to his feet.

"Good evening, Mrs. Armbrister," he said.

Mrs. Harriet Armbrister did not look back, and she left the huge drawing room without making a reply.

Aaron looked down at Sadie Anne. Her hands covered her face and her shoulders quivered. Aaron thought she was crying. He moved to the settee and sat beside her. He realized she was laughing.

Sadie Anne leaned back. "I didn't think I was going to make it. I almost laughed out loud."

"That would have been better than just sitting there," Aaron said irritably.

Sadie Anne laughed again and shook her head.

"I wish I could laugh," Aaron said.

"I'm sorry," she said, taking his hand. "I know how you feel about Mother. You have every right to dislike her."

Aaron leaned close to her. "We're together. That's all I care about."

She smiled at him. "I thought about you often."

"Even when you were in Europe?" he asked.

"Oh, that was horrible," Sadie Anne said. "Mother was ill the whole time. We stayed in a hotel for two months straight. I never saw a thing in Paris. And I was seasick on both crossings."

Aaron could not stop himself from touching her. He caressed her face as she spoke, then kissed her.

Sadie Anne laughed and pushed him away. "Aaron!"

Aaron stood. He looked around the room. All of the faces in the portraits were somber, seeming to stare down at him in disapproval.

"Which one is Wallace?" Aaron asked.

Sadie Anne pointed to a gilt-framed portrait over the fireplace. Aaron looked up at the bearded man in the painting, but could see little difference in him from the others in the room.

Aaron turned to Sadie Anne. "Let's get out of here."

"I'm not supposed to leave this room," she said.

"Good," Aaron said defiantly. He reached down and took Sadie Anne's hand. She giggled when he pulled her to her feet.

They tiptoed out of the drawing room. In the hallway they looked both ways in the exaggerated manner of theater actors. The hall was empty. High-stepping and laughing softly, they tiptoed to the big front door of the mansion.

They slipped outside into the cool of early evening. Aaron led Sadie Anne a short distance away from the door and embraced her.

"Oh, Aaron," Sadie Anne said.

Aaron kissed her long and hard. His passion mounted. He caressed her. Sadie Anne moaned and moved against him.

"Young man!"

Aaron jumped as he was startled by the sudden, commanding voice of Mrs. Harriet Armbrister.

"Take your filthy hands off my daughter!"

The frail-looking woman spoke with such force that Aaron released Sadie Anne and moved back a step.

"Mother—"

Mrs. Armbrister interrupted Sadie Anne by saying to Aaron, "How dare you lead my daughter out here and molest her."

"Oh, Mother, it was only a kiss," Sadie Anne said.

Mrs. Armbrister turned to her. "Next time . . . next time he'll force himself on you."

Aaron struggled with his own rage. "Mrs. Armbrister—"

The old woman pointed her bony index finger at him. "Young man, don't think for a moment I've forgotten you. I tried to warn Cleo about your kind—"

This time Aaron interrupted her. "I wish I could forget you."

Mrs. Armbrister shrieked, "How dare you!" She grabbed Sadie Anne's arm. Aaron was surprised to see her nearly fling Sadie Anne to the door.

"Leave my property, young man," Mrs. Armbrister said. "You will never set foot here again. I promise you that."

Sadie Anne protested, "Mother—"

Mrs. Armbrister took her arm and hauled her through the open doorway. The old woman glared back at Aaron, then slammed the great door.

Aaron felt enraged and powerless at once. He wanted to break into the mansion. He wanted to take Sadie Anne away from here. They were meant to be together. Aaron was certain of that. Only Mrs. Armbrister stood in their way.

Aaron reluctantly left the Armbrister mansion. As he walked home, an old fear rose up within him: He would never see Sadie Anne again.

The next morning a coach from the Armbrister mansion came down the hill, turned, and stopped in front of the Mills home. Aaron watched from his upstairs window as the driver came to the door. He heard a knock, then voices downstairs. A few minutes later Mrs. Mills left with the driver. He helped her into the coach, then climbed up to the seat and drove away.

In fifteen minutes the coach returned. The driver escorted Mrs. Mills to the door. A few minutes after the coach had gone, Aaron heard his mother come upstairs. She knocked on his door.

Aaron let her in. She looked at Aaron for a moment, then said, "Harriet tells me you have wronged her daughter."

"What did Sadie Anne tell you?" Aaron asked.

"I don't know why you keep calling her by that name," Mrs. Mills said. "Harriet calls her 'Cleo.'"

"She hates that name," Aaron said.

Mrs. Mills shrugged. "Well, that isn't the point, is it? I raised you to be a gentleman and now this happens."

"What has happened?"

"You tell me," Mrs. Mills said.

"I kissed her," Aaron said.

"Harriet's description of the way you had your hands on that girl sounds like more than a kiss to me."

"I did nothing wrong," Aaron said. "We kissed, that's all."

"Your hands were on that girl in an ungentlemanly way," Mrs. Mills said. She paused. "Oh, I know it's not all your fault. I'm sure she did not resist you. In fact, I would guess that she led you on."

"Mother," Aaron said, trying to control his rising anger, "I love her."

Mrs. Mills stared at him. "I know you think you do."

"I do love her," Aaron said. He thought, *I'll never love another woman so deeply, so completely.*

"Well, I won't argue the point," Mrs. Mills said. "Harriet tells me that she has forbidden you to set foot on the Armbrister property ever again. I believe that is best for all concerned."

Those last words echoed in Aaron's memory. His mother had used the same phrase summer before last when she learned that Sadie Anne would be going back East. Aaron was convinced that his mother had no understanding of his feelings—then or now.

"You must work on your studies," she went on. "There will be time for girls. Right now you should plan your future well."

"Mother, I will see Sadie Anne again," Aaron said.

Mrs. Mills looked at him. "How?"

"I don't know," he said. "I will, though."

Mrs. Mills stared at him. Aaron had defied her and now he met her stare. She began blinking rapidly. Aaron watched her turn and leave the room. Aaron realized he had won a battle of wills, a victory of some kind, but he felt no sense of exhilaration. He felt depressed.

Throughout the day Aaron stayed in his room. In the afternoon his tutor came and Aaron listened in silence to the man's recitation of the history of the

Roman Empire. The tutor left a reading assignment which Aaron ignored. In the evening he ate a silent meal with his mother. Jennifer had gone somewhere with Oliver Hayes. After the meal, Aaron returned to his room.

Aaron lay on his bed, staring at the ceiling when he heard voices downstairs. Someone had come to visit his mother. Fifteen or twenty minutes passed. Mrs. Mills came to the foot of the stairs and called Aaron.

Aaron left his bedroom and descended the stairs. He followed his mother into the living room. Sadie Anne was there.

Chapter V

"Hello, Aaron."

Aaron was too surprised to speak. Behind him, his mother said, "Aaron, will you walk this young lady home?"

Aaron nodded dumbly, took Sadie Anne by the hand, and led her outside. When he closed the front door, he stopped on the porch and faced Sadie Anne.

"What's going on?" he asked.

Sadie Anne said casually, "I came to visit your mother."

"Why?" Aaron asked.

"For some woman talk," she said, smiling.

"I don't understand," Aaron said.

"Walk me home, Aaron," Sadie Anne said.

They walked down the walk along Maple Avenue to Armbrister Street that led up Armbrister Hill.

"I told your mother the truth," Sadie Anne explained. "I suspected she got the wrong version of what happened last night. Your mother and I came to an understanding. I like her, Aaron."

Aaron did not say so aloud, but he understood none of this. Darkness shrouded the gate to the Armbrister mansion. Stained glass windows glowed at the end of the drive where the mansion loomed against the starry sky.

"I sneaked away," Sadie Anne said as they stopped at the gate. "I'll have to go in through the back."

Aaron moved close to her and embraced her. "Sadie Anne, run away with me."

She laughed softly.

"I mean it," Aaron said.

"Shhhhh," she whispered in his ear. "Tomorrow night we can be together."

"Where?" Aaron asked.

"In back there is a summerhouse," Sadie Anne said. "You can't see it from here—"

"I know where it is," Aaron said.

The eagerness in his voice made her laugh softly again. "Meet me there," she said. "About nine."

Aaron kissed her, or tried to. In the darkness the kiss was poorly aimed. He kissed the side of her nose, then found her mouth, open and warm.

Sadie Anne broke the embrace. She turned away and walked hurriedly up the drive, angling off across the lawn. Aaron saw her pass through a patch of yellow light cast through a window, then disappear.

The next day passed with agonizing slowness. In desperation, Aaron tried to work at his studies and he actually listened to his tutor's lecture in the afternoon.

During the evening meal few words passed between Aaron and his mother. Again, Jennifer had gone somewhere with Oliver. Mrs. Mills made no mention of Sadie Anne's visit last night. Aaron was painfully curious to know what had been said, but he did not ask. The best policy, he had learned from experience, was to leave well enough alone.

Before nine o'clock Aaron's mother went upstairs to her bedroom and closed the door. Aaron blew out the downstairs lamps and quietly left the house. In the darkness he climbed Armbrister Hill to the stand of pine trees and he walked through the trees to the iron fence. Aaron felt his way along the fence until he found a low place. He crawled under.

Aaron walked up the sloping lawn toward the darkened mansion. By starlight he saw the dim outline of the summerhouse. When he reached the frame building with screened sides, he walked around it until he found the screen door. Hinges squealed when he slowly pulled the door open.

"Aaron?" Sadie Anne's voice came out of the dark interior of the summerhouse.

"Yes."

"Over here," she said.

Aaron's eyes slowly adjusted to the dim light. In the center of the summerhouse stood an octagonal table. Frame folding chairs were scattered about. Aaron worked his way around the table, almost knocked over a chair, but caught it, and then he saw a long, rounded form at the base of a wall. Aaron knelt down. He found Sadie Anne reclining on a blanket. Aaron whispered her name. Sadie Anne pulled him down on top of her, wrapping her soft but strong arms around him.

They parted in an hour, each promising the other to meet here tomorrow night. They lingered over a last kiss. Aaron released Sadie Anne and watched her enter the mansion through a back door near the adjoining carriage house. Aaron left the grounds the way he had come, carefully working his way down the steep, weed-grown hillside to his backyard. A lamp burned in the window of his mother's bedroom.

Aaron entered the house and climbed the creaking

stairs. When he reached the hall, he was surprised to see no light streaming out under the door of his mother's bedroom. She had blown out the lamp.

The secret meetings between Aaron and Sadie Anne continued through the month in the pattern that was established that first night. How secret the meetings were became a matter of speculation with Aaron. He suspected his mother knew, even though she never mentioned it to him. Aaron pursued his studies with some diligence, and his mother seemed pleased with the reports she received from the tutor.

At least one maid in the Armbrister mansion knew of the meetings in the summerhouse. Aaron learned from Sadie Anne how she deceived Mrs. Armbrister. Sadie Anne would retire to her bedroom about eight-thirty every night. Before nine o'clock a maid would take her place in the canopied bed while Sadie Anne slipped out of the mansion through the service entrance. Should Mrs. Armbrister look into her daughter's bedroom, she would think the still form she saw was that of her sleeping daughter.

Late in July Jennifer became engaged to Oliver Hayes. Round, thick spectacles enlarged Oliver's eyes and gave him an owlish look, and he had a peculiar way of always seeming amused. Perhaps he thought he was being pleasant. Aaron felt uncomfortable around the man and wondered what Jennifer saw in him. But Aaron wondered what Oliver could possibly see in Jennifer that would inspire him to court her, too.

These matters scarcely troubled Aaron. He was so enraptured with Sadie Anne that he could not imagine anyone else experiencing such intense emotions.

One night as they left the summerhouse, Sadie

Anne gave Aaron a small package and made him promise not to open it until he got home. The gift was a thin rectangle. At first Aaron thought it was a small book, perhaps a volume of poetry. If they were love poems, Aaron decided, he would memorize one and recite it for her.

But when Aaron opened the package in his room that night, he found that Sadie Anne had given him a photographic portrait of herself. In the picture Sadie Anne stood before a studio mountain scene, demurely looking off to one side. She wore a light dress with puffed sleeves and she held a parasol in her right hand. No matter how Aaron turned the photograph, he could not meet her eyes.

The pose was proper for a young lady, Aaron supposed, but this one did not do justice to Sadie Anne. But then again, Aaron thought, no photographer could capture the essence of the woman he loved.

Aaron spoke of marriage to Sadie Anne one night in the summerhouse.

"We're secret lovers," she whispered.

"I want you for my wife," Aaron said.

"You're not ready for a wife, are you, Aaron?" she asked.

"I'm ready for you," Aaron said. "Marry me and we'll go away together."

"Where?" she asked.

Aaron had not thought far enough ahead to have a ready answer. "Anywhere," he blurted.

"What about your education?" Sadie Anne asked.

"I can be educated anywhere," Aaron said. He thought a moment. "I'll get a job as a printer."

Sadie Anne fell silent.

"We'll be happy as long as we're together," Aaron said.

"You'd come to hate me," she whispered.

Alarmed, Aaron said, "Don't talk that way. I could never hate you."

Sadie Anne stood.

Aaron scrambled to his feet. He tried to see Sadie Anne's expression in the darkness, but could not. "We should talk about our future. We should make plans."

"Future," Sadie Anne said dully. "Yours and mine."

"What do you mean?" Aaron asked.

"Just that," Sadie Anne said, moving away from him. "You have yours. I have mine."

The hinges of the summerhouse door squealed as Sadie Anne opened the door and went out. Aaron followed.

"Good night," Sadie Anne whispered over her shoulder, and strode to the back door of the mansion.

The next night Sadie Anne did not come to the summerhouse. Aaron waited more than an hour, then walked home down the back hillside to his house. He spent a nearly sleepless night, telling himself that nothing was wrong, yet knowing something was.

The next night Aaron found Sadie Anne waiting for him at the door of the summerhouse. He embraced her and kissed her. She did not resist. Worse, she did not respond. Aaron peered at her face in the darkness.

"Aaron, you must not come here anymore," she said.

He was too stunned to reply for a moment. "Why?"

Sadie Anne shook her head. "I can't talk about it—ever."

"Can't talk about what?" Aaron asked. When she made no reply, Aaron grasped her by the arms.

"Aaron, don't," she said.

"I love you," Aaron said. "Do you love me?" After a long moment, he demanded, "Answer me."

"Aaron, I don't want to hurt you."

"How can love hurt?" he asked.

Sadie Anne said, "Love can hurt worse than anything."

"I don't understand what you're saying," Aaron said.

"You're innocent," she said. "I thought you could make me an innocent. But you can't. I am still who I am."

"What are you talking about?"

"I can't escape myself," she said. She turned away and walked toward the mansion.

Aaron went after her. He grabbed her arm, but Sadie Anne pulled away.

"Aaron, good-by," she said. "Your love was the greatest gift I've ever received." She moved quickly to the mansion door and went inside, closing the door after her.

Aaron stood outside, trying to make sense out of what had happened. Then he rushed to the door, determined to enter the mansion, find Sadie Anne, and demand an explanation. She owed him one. He turned the door handle and pulled. The door was bolted.

Aaron's frustration turned to anger. He looked through the glass in the door. Down the long hall he saw light streaming out of an arched doorway. Aaron walked around the side of the mansion to the huge stained glass windows off the drawing room. The colorful windows were ringed with narrow borders of clear glass. Aaron came close and peered through one.

In the drawing room he saw a strange sight. Mrs.

Armbrister sat on the upholstered settee. In front of her stood a tall man with flowing white hair. He held an open Bible in one hand, gestured with his other, as though delivering a hellfire sermon. By the fireplace, beneath the portrait of Wallace Armbrister, was a stocky young man. Bright red hair stood out from his head in a wild manner. His expression remained blank while the white-haired man carried on a lengthy tirade.

Aaron heard the man's voice, but could not not understand his words. Then Mrs. Armbrister, shaking her head violently, spoke to the man. She got to her feet, waved a bony fist at the white-haired man, then left the drawing room.

Aaron saw the white-haired man throw the Bible to the carpeted floor. Beyond, the stocky young man absently rubbed his eyes with one fleshy hand. Aaron realized he was mentally deficient.

Presently the white-haired man stooped down and picked up his Bible. He walked out of the drawing room, followed by the young man. The young man had a curious way of walking. He waddled.

Aaron backed away from the window. He felt as though he had watched a strange dream, a nightmare that began when Sadie Anne had left him.

Aaron walked home. He felt confused, but determined to return tomorrow morning and find out what was going on. Aaron slept fitfully that night. He awakened early and looked out his window at a pink sky. He went downstairs and made breakfast for himself. His mind was busy with theories about why Sadie Anne had acted the way she had. None were satisfactory. Aaron held out a remote hope that Sadie Anne would be regretful and they would make up and she would agree to marry him.

Aaron's thoughts were interrupted by a loud knocking on the front door. Aaron walked down the front hall and answered the door before either Jennifer or his mother were awakened.

A policeman stood on the porch. "Mr. Aaron Mills?"

"Yes."

"City Marshal Ross Hogan wants to see you," he said. "Right away."

"What about?" Aaron asked.

"Come with me, please," the policeman said. He looked at Aaron for a moment, then said, "You might want to get dressed."

Aaron wore only a nightshirt. He suddenly felt cold and embarrassed. "What's this all about?"

"Marshal Hogan will tell you," the young policeman said. "Do you want to get dressed?"

Aaron nodded. "I'll be right back."

The policeman stepped into the hall before Aaron could close the door. "I'll come along."

"Why?" Aaron asked.

"Procedure," he said.

"I wish you'd tell me what this is all about," Aaron said.

The uniformed policeman said nothing. Aaron turned around and walked down the short hallway to the stairs. The policeman came along behind. He followed Aaron up the stairs and waited outside the bedroom door while he dressed.

As Aaron pulled on his boots, he had a sudden mental image of what might happen if either his sister or mother came out of her room while the policeman stood in the upstairs hall. The imagined scene was a comical one, belying his fear.

Aaron and the policeman quietly left the house.

The sky was bright with the early morning sun. Birds sang high in the trees on Maple Avenue. The policeman ushered Aaron into the back of a police van and locked the door, no doubt in accordance with "procedure."

Aaron looked out of the small, barred window as the van swung around in the middle of the street and went to the corner. There the van turned right and ascended Armbrister Hill.

The police van turned and entered the Armbrister mansion drive. Aaron was surprised to see several buggies and saddle horses. Near the steps stood an ambulance.

The policeman let Aaron out of the van. They walked up the steps to the front door of the mansion. The great door stood open. In the entryway Aaron saw several men with note pads and pencils in their hands. As Aaron and the policeman came in, a bald man in a white frock coat rushed past on his way outside. He carried a small black bag. The front of his coat was bloodstained.

The men who clogged the hallway pursued the man like birds after prey. They shouted questions, but received no answers. The bald man went out onto the portico and shouted for the ambulance to be brought around to the back entrance.

Aaron and the policeman were momentarily surrounded by the men in the front hall. They were journalists, Aaron realized, and they bombarded him with questions about who he was and why he was here. At that moment Aaron did not know the answer to either question. He was dazed.

The young policeman took Aaron by the arm and bulled his way through the tightening knot of journalists. Aaron and the policeman hurried down the hall, ducking under a rope that apparently kept everyone else out.

Aaron was led to the far end of the hall. At the mansion's rear entrance the hall turned left, leading to a back staircase.

Aaron stopped short. At the base of the carved newel post sprawled the frail body of Mrs. Harriet Armbrister. She was nude, lying in a dried pool of blood. Her skull was split open and her lifeless eyes stared up at the ceiling. Aaron turned away and vomited.

Chapter VI

"Keep that body covered!"

Through tearing eyes Aaron saw the man who had come down the staircase and shouted. He appeared to be a man in his sixties, gray-haired, and he wore a walrus mustache. Aaron wiped his eyes. He then saw the badge of the Denver City Marshal on the man's vest.

A fat policeman who stood near the corpse of Mrs. Harriet Armbrister protested, "I had it covered, Marshal. The goddamn coroner came in and uncovered it. He says he wants it moved downtown."

"Not yet," the marshal said irritably. He pointed to a sheet at the base of the stairs. "Cover it." He turned his attention to Aaron. "Who are you?"

Before Aaron could clear his throat and speak, the young policeman said, "He's Aaron Mills, Marshal."

The marshal came closer to Aaron. "Are you all right, son?"

Aaron nodded.

"Come out here," the marshal said, taking Aaron by the arm. He led Aaron outside through the rear entrance. "Take a breath of fresh air. I'm Ross Hogan. I'm in charge of this investigation—supposed to be, anyhow. I didn't aim for you to be hauled in there to

look at a sight like that. It turned my stomach, too."
He paused. "I've got a few questions to ask you. Feel
up to answering?"

Aaron nodded. He tried to speak, but couldn't. He
coughed wetly.

"Did you recognize the deceased?"

Aaron cleared his throat. "Mrs. Armbrister."

"When did you last see her?" Hogan asked.

Aaron's memory flashed back to last night. "Where's
Sadie Anne?"

"Just answer my questions for the time being,"
Hogan said. He repeated the question.

Aaron looked at the city marshal and saw deep-
ening lines at the corners of his eyes. Aaron sensed
that he knew.

"Last night."

Hogan was obviously surprised. "Last night?
Where?"

Aaron described the scene he had observed in the
drawing room. He explained that he had visited
Sadie Anne in the summerhouse too.

Hogan nodded. "I knew all about that. One of the
Armbrister maids was gone for the day. She came
back this morning and found the murdered women.
She told us all about your meetings with the girl out
there." He pointed to the summerhouse.

"Is Sadie Anne . . . ?" Aaron's voice trailed off.

"The girl?" Hogan asked. "She ain't dead. Not
here, anyhow. She's gone. Ran off."

Aaron shook his head. "No . . ."

"We're still piecing this thing together," Hogan
said. "The old lady and three maids were murdered
last night. All of them killed with an axe, the way
I figure. All of them stripped naked. Worst killings I
ever seen."

Hogan studied Aaron. "Show me how you came up here every night."

Aaron led the city marshal past the summerhouse to the low place beneath the iron fence. Aaron was surprised to see several policemen in the trees.

"Find anything?" Hogan asked the policeman nearest the fence.

"No, sir," he answered. "We worked our way all the way down the hill, like you said."

Hogan turned to Aaron. "When I first heard about you, Aaron, you were my suspect. I figured if you had killed those women, you'd have got splattered with blood and buried your clothes on the way home. But after talking to you, I can see you didn't have nothing to do with this killing. You ain't the type. Whoever did it is plumb out of his head. Besides, the maid went through the house and found some of the daughter's clothes missing. The wall safe had been opened by the combination. She must have been in on it."

"No," Aaron said. "I can't believe that."

"Were you in love with her?" Hogan asked.

Aaron nodded.

"Well, you might have misjudged her," Hogan said. "Wouldn't be the first time for a young man."

"No," Aaron said again.

"Don't be so sure," Hogan said. He looked back toward the mansion. "Aaron, I'm going to save you a pile of trouble."

Aaron didn't understand. "What?"

"This story is likely to be the biggest one around this town for a long time," Hogan said. "I can save you from being hounded by every newspaperman in Denver, not to mention other parts of the country, by keeping your name a secret. All you got to do is crawl under this fence and go on home. If I have any more questions to ask you, I know where to find you."

Aaron nodded.

"Go on, now," Hogan said.

"Thank you," Aaron said. He dropped to his knees and crawled under the iron fence.

Hogan said, "One more thing, Mills. If that girl friend of yours ever looks you up, or if you ever hear from her, you come tell me. Give me your word on that."

Aaron looked at Marshal Hogan through the fence. "You have my word."

"All right," Ross Hogan said. "Go on home now."

Aaron walked into the trees, turned, and took one last look at the mansion and the summerhouse, then he hiked down the hill. The policemen were gone.

Aaron was met in the kitchen by his mother and sister.

"Aaron, what's wrong?" Mrs. Mills asked. "The police were here, asking all sorts of questions."

Aaron felt tired and dizzy. He sat in a chair and told them what he had seen and what Marshal Hogan had told him. Both women were shocked.

"But surely they don't suspect you had anything to do with it," Mrs. Mills said.

Aaron shook his head. "Not now. The marshal did before he talked to me."

Surprisingly, Jennifer was outraged. "The very idea! How dare they accuse you!"

Aaron looked at his sister and smiled at her. Her expression of outrage changed to one of affection.

Throughout the following week Aaron read newspaper accounts of the murders in the Armbrister mansion. The story was front page news in Denver and the major newspapers throughout the country.

Only sparse facts were ever reported. Most accounts agreed that none of the doors had been forced open. A wall safe behind the portrait of Wallace Armbrister had been opened by combination, but no one was able to determine what had been stolen. Mrs. Armbrister had been secretive about her possessions.

The coroner was widely quoted. He said the murderer had wielded an axe or large hatchet. The size of the wounds indicated that the murderer had been quite strong, too.

Even the *Police Gazette* published a sensationalized account of the murders. The halls of the mansion were described as being "blood-splashed and fairly echoing the helpless and hopeless screams of the dying women." The Armbrister family, said the *Gazette* writer, was "tragedy-ridden" and "haunted by a past of violent deaths, beginning with Wallace Armbrister's suicide." In conclusion, the *Gazette* suggested that the murderer might be a "mystery paramour," who ran off with Mrs. Armbrister's adopted daughter. With a shock, Aaron realized the description might be of him.

No reporters came to the Mills home, so apparently Hogan had been true to his word in not releasing Aaron's name.

Two weeks later Hogan still had not come to talk to Aaron. Aaron was eager to know if any new clues had been found, and he wondered what Hogan's theories were as to the murderer's identify.

Then, the day before school started, Aaron saw Marshal Hogan's name in the *Rocky Mountain News*. He had been shot. Hogan had tried to break up a fight in a Denver saloon and had been shot through the leg. He had bled seriously, but was recovering.

Aaron attended freshman classes in the exclusive Denver College for Men. Aaron was never interviewed by Marshal Hogan or by anyone from the city marshal's office. The next time he saw Hogan's name in the newspaper was late in October. After recovering from the severe leg wound, Hogan had retired from office. He was honored by the mayor for outstanding service to the city of Denver.

Aaron's first year at Denver College set the pattern for all four years of his higher education. Aaron threw himself into his classwork. He studied constantly. Every night he worked in the college library, and every weekend he studied at home. By the end of his freshman year Aaron had made a name for himself as the outstanding scholar in his class.

In the summer Jennifer married Oliver Hayes. After the ceremony Aaron observed that his mother appeared to be happy for Jennifer, but when the new Mr. and Mrs. Hayes announced they were moving to Sacramento, California, where Oliver would work as a clerk for a judge, Mrs. Mills failed to conceal her sadness. She had lost her daughter.

Aaron attended classes throughout the summer months, too. He spent more time at the college than he did at home. Next year he did well in all of his classes, but he excelled in the subjects of literature and English language.

At the beginning of his junior year, Aaron was appointed to the position of editor-in-chief of the school newspaper, the *Avalanche*. Aaron held this post in addition to a heavy study load. He cut short his sleep to make up for lost study time. And at year's end he still finished at the top of his class.

As a senior, Aaron was reappointed to the position of editor-in-chief of the *Avalanche*, becoming the first student in the college's history to hold the job for two consecutive years. Politically, Aaron became interested in the Populist movement. He wrote one editorial in favor of a graduated federal income tax, then he wrote another advocating the nationalization of all the country's railroads. At this point the college president called Aaron into his office and informed him that the *Avalanche* could not be used as a forum to promote radical ideas. The college president showed Aaron a sheaf of letters. All were complaints from college donors.

Aaron graduated magna cum laude in May 1898. Mrs. Mills watched from the audience as Aaron received graduation honors. Following the ceremonies, several professors sought Aaron out and recommended that he continue his education. Aaron should become a professor himself, they said, and pass along his academic zeal to students.

Mrs. Mills was delighted with these suggestions. As she rode home with her son in the Mills family carriage that afternoon, she told Aaron to take those suggestions to heart. He would make a fine professor. She would be proud of him.

Strangely, the graduation ceremony had left Aaron exhausted and saddened, not triumphant. He felt as though he had reached the end of a career. Thoughts of the future troubled him.

"It'll be a long time before I go into another classroom, Mother," Aaron said.

She stared at him. "Well, what are your plans?"

Aaron shrugged and looked out of the carriage window. "I have none."

Aaron realized he had left Denver College without making a single friendship. He had given himself no time for a social life. As editor-in-chief of the

Avalanche, Aaron had held himself aloof from his assistant editors and reporters. He had regarded them more as employees than as fellow students. Aaron now regretted his behavior.

After arriving home, Aaron went upstairs to his room. He felt very tired. He thought he could sleep, but as he lay on his bed, eyes closed, his mind unexpectedly conjured up a clear image of Sadie Anne. He saw her on the portico of the Armbrister mansion. She came toward him, promising warmth and satisfaction without ever saying a word, and then her lips parted. Aaron wanted to hear her speak, but could not.

In an odd way, Sadie Anne was responsible for Aaron's academic achievements. As a teen-ager, he'd learned a valuable lesson when he had worked in his father's shop. The long hours and strenuous labor had given Aaron an escape from the lovelorn sadness he had felt over losing Sadie Anne. Hard, relentless work in college had achieved the same result.

Only now could Aaron admit this truth to himself. In college he had almost convinced himself that social events were a waste of time. The laughing young men who were out sparking the ladies every night could be better spending their time by working at their studies, Aaron had told himself. And as if to prove the point, Aaron worked relentlessly. Now Aaron suspected those young classmates of his were better prepared to face the future than he.

Deep down Aaron always wondered what had happened to Sadie Anne. Such thoughts troubled him, and when they came upon him before he slept, he invariably dreamed of her. Sometimes he dreamed that Sadie Anne had been kidnapped. Other dreams flashed back to the mansion and the corpse of Mrs. Harriet Armbrister. From these dreams Aaron awoke in a sweat.

At noon of the next day opportunity knocked on the door of the Mills home. This opportunity came in the person of Homer Witt, founder and editor-in-chief of the *Denver City Journal*. The *Journal* was a progressive newspaper that advocated Witt's brand of Populism mixed with his dreams for a utopian society. Witt editorially advocated such radical social causes as trial marriage, abolishment of prisons, and communal living. These latter experiments in living would be, as weather permitted, nudist.

When Homer Witt introduced himself, Aaron immediately recalled a remark Witt was said to have made in defense of communal living. "No man or woman can tell a lie while naked."

Chapter VII

Aaron knew Homer Witt only by reputation. He was Denver's firebrand. Little more than a year ago Witt had editorially labeled Denver's mayor "a crook of the first water." The epithet was meant to be taken literally. A construction company in which the mayor was a principal stockholder built a faulty bridge over Cherry Creek. The bridge had been in service a month when it crashed into the river under the weight of three freight wagons. The contract to replace the bridge was reissued by the mayor to his own construction company.

Homer Witt exposed this corruption in headline fashion. The mayor replied by ordering Witt's arrest. The charges proved to be empty ones, and Witt was out of jail by suppertime. The next issue of the *Journal* carried a message in half-inch type on its front page: "MAN TELLS THE TRUTH AND GOES TO JAIL FOR HIS TROUBLE. THE CROOK OF THE FIRST WATER STILL SWIMS IN DENVER'S GUTTERS. JUSTICE, WHERE ART THOU?" Within a month the mayor resigned.

"I'm Aaron Mills," Aaron said, reaching out to meet Witt's hand.

"I know who you are," Homer Witt said, shaking Aaron's hand vigorously. "I read an editorial of yours last year that impressed me. I agreed with you then, and although I've changed my views some, I still believe some form of Populism is the wave of the future. And it's a wave we'd better ride." He took a breath and added, "I'm surprised Denver College allowed you to publish such notions."

"They never did again," Aaron said, grinning.

Witt laughed heartily. "Time brings change, and no matter what the rich old conservatives say, time can't be bought. And I believe that if we don't do something to spread the wealth in this country, we'll become a nation of aristocrats and tramps."

Aaron felt overwhelmed by this man. He had no sooner shaken hands than he had delivered a political speech. Aaron was amused and interested at once. Witt's appearance befitted his manner. He was bear-sized. Thick cinnamon hair was combed straight back from his face. He had amazingly thick eyebrows that jumped as he spoke, seeming to add emphasis to his words.

"Come in," Aaron said, realizing he was slow to show courtesy to this man.

Witt stepped in the hall and then followed Aaron into the sitting room. Aaron caught a glimpse of his mother as she ducked through the archway that opened into the dining room. Aaron sensed that his mother was somewhere back there, listening.

"I didn't come here to talk politics," Homer Witt said. "I'm here to offer you a position."

Aaron was surprised. "A position?"

"That's right," Witt said. His eyebrows jumped. "Unless you've already accepted one with someone else."

"Oh, no," Aaron said, too quickly.

Homer Witt smiled. "I need a young man of your background—and intelligence. I spoke to one of your professors yesterday. He told me that a student of your caliber comes along once in a lifetime. He expressed the hope that you'll continue your education."

Aaron shook his head. "I've had enough of school."

"Well, I'm glad to hear that," Witt said. He paused. "I'm here to offer you an editorship."

"What?" Aaron exclaimed.

"Let me back up a minute and tell you what I'm trying to accomplish with the *Journal*," Witt said. "I've been accused of being a yellow journalist, and I've probably been guilty of the charge a time or two. I've run that paper for twenty-five years, and I reckon I've made my share of mistakes. But that's in the past. Now I want to change the format of the *Journal*. From now on, the paper will look and read more like a traditional newspaper. I've hired some new reporters who will write straight news. There won't be any more advertising on the front page. The second page will still run my editorials, but I've decided to be less adamant, you might say." His eyebrows bobbed rapidly. "The third page will be turned over to society news. And I want you for my society news editor."

"Me?" Aaron asked, feeling foolish as he spoke.

"Now, don't be overpowered by the title," Homer Witt said. "You'll be an editor, all right, probably the youngest in the state, but you'll be doing your own legwork. You know where to go and who to talk to. Well, what do you say?"

"I don't know what to say," Aaron said. "I'm not sure I'm the man for the job. I haven't had much experience."

"You've had enough as far as I'm concerned," Witt

said. "I keep an eye on the *Avalanche*. You've improved that little paper in the last two years. With your skill, I expect you to give the *Journal* the best society page in town."

Aaron smiled. "You're very persuasive, Mr. Witt."

"I hope so," he said. He stood. "Why don't you think over my offer for a couple of days, Aaron. Come to my office and I'll show you around. Then you can make a decision."

Aaron stood and faced him. "I can tell you right now that I'd like to work for you, Mr. Witt."

"Well, good—"

"But I foresee one problem," Aaron said.

"What?" Witt asked.

"I wouldn't be satisfied writing society news for the rest of my life," Aaron said.

"I can understand that." Witt said, "and I appreciate your candor. What are your other interests?"

"I've always been intrigued with crime reporting," Aaron said.

"I see," Witt said. He thought a moment. "Well, let's see if we can strike a compromise here. For the next half year or so, I imagine you'll have your hands full with the society page. You'll have to start from scratch. But after you get things rolling, some of the legwork could be delegated to a reporter. That would give you some time to work the police beat. I've just hired a man away from the *Rocky Mountain News* who is Denver's top crime writer—Sam Catton. Six or eight months from now, I'll assign you to work with Sam. You'll be learning from the best. How does that sound to you?"

"Fine," Aaron said.

"Then we have a deal?" Witt asked.

"Yes, sir," Aaron said.

"Come to work on Monday," Witt said, shaking Aaron's hand like a pump handle. "Welcome to the *Denver City Journal!*"

Aaron walked Homer Witt to the front door and saw him out. When Aaron closed the door and turned around, he saw his mother. She stood in the hallway, weeping.

Aaron went to her. "Mother, what's wrong?"

She looked up with reddened eyes. "Why did you tell that madman you'll work for him?"

"Mother, he's not mad—"

"You know his reputation as well as I do," she said with surprising sharpness. She wiped her eyes with a lace handkerchief. "Why didn't you discuss this with me? You know I want you to go into a real profession."

"I want to be a journalist," Aaron said.

In an unguarded moment her lips tightened. She scoffed at Aaron. "Yesterday you said you didn't know what you wanted to do. You said you had no plans."

Aaron felt his face grow hot with embarrassment and anger. "I should have said that I knew what I didn't want. I don't want to be a professor. I don't want to be a doctor or lawyer."

"You're just tired of school," she said. "Aaron, give yourself some time before you make a decision. Go to that man and tell him you need time to think—"

Aaron interrupted her. "No, Mother."

Mrs. Mills looked at her son for a long moment. "You're every bit as stubborn as your father was."

"Father did well," Aaron said. "He was a good man."

She nodded and suppressed a sob. "He worked too hard."

"He worked hard for us," Aaron said.

She shook her head slowly. "Your father worked himself to death."

Monday morning Aaron began his career in journalism. He caught a yellow trolley car downtown and walked three blocks to the red brick, two-story building that housed the pressroom and offices of the *Denver City Journal.* Aaron was greeted enthusiastically by Homer Witt. Witt gave Aaron a thorough tour of the building, from the basement coal chute to the pressroom on the main floor, and the offices upstairs.

In the pressroom Aaron saw sights and smelled odors that reminded him strongly of his father's shop. He even saw a scrawny youth sweeping the floor while the aproned shop foreman looked on.

But upstairs Aaron saw sights he had never seen before. The main, outer office was crowded with desks, most manned by reporters who had just received their assignments from the city editor. The city editor was a plump, surly-looking man named Henry Daniels. Daniels gave Aaron a brisk handshake and a curt glance as Witt introduced them. Homer Witt took the occasion to explain that Aaron would report directly to Witt himself, not to the city editor. Aaron suspected Daniels had somehow taken offense at this arrangement.

The reporters, eight or ten that Aaron met that day, worked like bees in a hive. Many were on their way out the door as Witt introduced Aaron to them. Afterward, the names jumbled in Aaron's mind, but he did note that one man was absent—Sam Catton.

Along the back wall of the outer office were three doors that led to private offices. The center one belonged to Homer Witt. His name was lettered in gold and black paint in the middle of the door panel. To the right Aaron saw on a half-opened door Henry Daniels' name. On the last door Aaron looked twice. He saw his own name, printed in bold gold and black letters: AARON MILLS, EDITOR, SOCIAL NEWS.

"How does that look to you?" Homer Witt asked.

"I wasn't expecting this," Aaron said.

"Take a look inside," Witt said.

Aaron opened the door and stepped in. The office was scarcely larger than a broom closet, and it was dominated by a flat-topped oak desk and an oak filing cabinet against one wall. A swivel chair was behind the desk.

Aaron turned back to Witt. "I like it."

Witt grinned, eyebrows bobbing up and down. "Good." He looked at his pocket watch. "I have to meet with my city editor now. In half an hour come into my office and we'll get started on the mechanics of the *Journal's* society page. I want to have the first issue on the street with Thursday's edition. Can we do it?"

"Yes, sir," Aaron said.

Witt nodded and smiled. "See you in half an hour."

Aaron closed the office door and cautiously moved around the desk. He sat in the swivel chair. The spring squeaked under his weight. Aaron ran his hands over the smooth desk top, then opened all of the drawers. They were empty, ready for him.

Aaron's work habits in college carried over to his job. He was the first to arrive every morning, and he was usually the last to leave at night. Aaron worked closely with Homer Witt. They designed a page heading and determined the sizes and kinds of type to be used. On Wednesday Aaron spoke to enough people on Capitol Hill and Armbrister Hill to rough out a schedule of social events for the coming week and mention the activities of several families.

On Thursday the first issue of the *Denver City Journal* hit the streets with Aaron's name on the masthead. Aaron felt like celebrating, but had no one to celebrate with. He had not worked with any of the reporters, and the city editor had plainly taken a dislike to him. Aaron's only friend was the editor-in-chief, Homer Witt.

Witt had been surprised at Aaron's detailed knowledge of printing. Aaron explained that he had worked as a printer's devil in his father's shop one summer.

"You learned well," Witt said. He added, "I've always believed it is a good thing for a young man to have knowledge of a trade. Keeps his feet on the ground."

Aaron remembered hearing his own father say almost the same words.

Aaron established a beat in the Capitol and Armbrister Hill sections of Denver. He knocked on the same doors that he had politely rapped upon when he had escorted his mother and sister around these neighborhoods. Aaron had retained at least a nodding acquaintance with nearly all of the families listed in Denver's social register, and he soon learned that most of them were eager for public mention, even in a newspaper as controversial as the *Denver City Journal*.

A few weeks before Christmas that year, Jennifer wrote from Sacramento, California, that she was an expectant mother. The birth would take place in June. Aaron spent Christmas Day with his mother, the first full day he had been with her since he had started working. He noticed his mother seemed distant and preoccupied. Then on the evening of that day she announced she planned to sell the house and move to Sacramento.

"Jennifer needs me," she said.

Aaron was surprised. "Are you sure you want to sell the house, Mother? You might want to come back someday."

She shook her head slowly and said, "I'll never come back here." She looked around the sitting room. "I must go where I am needed."

Aaron packed up his belongings over the holidays. He discarded his boyhood toys, among them a red fire engine powered by a heavy flywheel. He had run the fire engine across the floor of his room many times, rushing to imaginary fires. Of his childhood accumulations, Aaron saved only his baby spoon and a few mounted photographs of the family. Aaron lingered over a photographic portrait of his father. He recalled his mother saying he was every bit as stubborn as his father. Aaron knew he was as hard a worker as his father, and he wondered if he shared other traits.

While emptying his clothes dresser, Aaron found some items that stirred memories. He found the portrait that Sadie Anne had given him, and the note she had written when she had gone back East to finishing school. Aaron found he could hardly bear to look at the photograph. He did not read the note again. He tossed them both in an open suitcase.

He found his hidden collection of dime novels and *Police Gazettes*, too. Looking through them now made Aaron feel older than he was. What had once fired his imagination now seemed childish. And after reading the account of the murders in the Armbrister mansion, he knew there was little truth in the *Gazette.*

Aaron moved into a frame boarding house located half a dozen city blocks from the *Denver City Journal* building. The room was sparsely furnished with a tarnished brass bed and commode and one ladder-back chair. The clothes closet was only an iron bar suspended from the ceiling, covered by a curtain.

Aaron got caught up in the current bicycle rage. He purchased a green two-wheeler called "The Green Machine." For the next several days Aaron rode his bicycle to work, dodging wagon and carriage traffic and the lumbering yellow electric streetcars. Aaron found he could enter the alley behind the *Journal* and open the back door near the coal chute and set his machine inside. At the boarding house he kept his Green Machine in his room. But in mid-January snows fell. From then until winter broke Aaron traveled in streetcars and on foot.

Early in the spring Mrs. Mills sold the house on Maple Avenue. Aaron helped her pack all of her china and silver and other valued possessions into wooden boxes and large trunks with brass corners. Aaron borrowed a neighbor's flatbed wagon and hauled all of the boxes and trunks to Union Station. Aaron shipped them to his sister's address in California. A week later Aaron took his mother to the station and saw her off on a westbound train.

Their moment of parting was curiously formal and unemotional. Aaron kissed his mother and then helped her board the coach. Down the line, the locomotive's whistle blew twice. Aaron stood outside the coach his mother sat in. She peered soberly out of the window at him. The coach began to move in small jerks. Mrs. Mills raised her hand as the train slid away from the station. Aaron realized she was crying.

Chapter VIII

The second week in April Homer Witt came into Aaron's office. He sat on the corner of Aaron's desk. "I seem to recall a deal we made when you came to work here."

For a moment Aaron's mind went blank.

"Are you still interested in crime writing?" Witt prompted.

Aaron smiled. "Yes, sir." In truth he had been so caught up with the demands of his job, he still thought of Witt's promise to assign him to the crime beat as far off in the future. The future had sneaked up on Aaron.

"You've kept your end of the deal," Witt said. "The *Journal's* society page has turned out to be everything I expected it to be. The social calendar we run is the most complete in town, and we have more news about Denver society than any paper in town. Our circulation is up. I give you a great deal of the credit.

Aaron said, "Thank you." He added, "But I think your ideas about changing the format of the newspaper are responsible for increased circulation."

"Perhaps so," Witt said, "but you helped bring my ideas to life." He clapped his hands together. "Well, enough backslapping today. Let's get to the business at hand. Starting Monday, I want you to write down your regular work schedule. I'll have Daniels assign your beat to a reporter. He will turn his stories in to you. You will be responsible for getting your page in by deadline, as before. But now you should have some free time. I'll put you to work with Sam Catton." Witt stood, "Come into my office Monday morning with your work schedule. I'll introduce you to Sam then."

Aaron knew Sam Catton only by sight. Catton rarely came into the main office to work at his desk. Generally, his stories were delivered to the city editor's basket by a teenaged girl.

Sam Catton was middle-aged. He was a slope-shouldered man who often appeared to have slept in his clothes. Catton had the reputation of being a heavy drinker and a gambler. Around the *Journal* office Aaron had overheard snatches of stories about the man. Last Saint Patrick's Day Catton had entered the annual beer drinking contest in a downtown saloon called Murphy's Exchange. The saloon, noted for the violent nature of its clientele, was locally known as the "Slaughterhouse."

Sam Catton won the contest by guzzling four quarts of green-colored beer in two minutes. He collected his winnings, then retired to a back table, where he wrote out the day's copy as though nothing out of the ordinary had taken place.

Aaron had seen the girl who delivered Catton's copy many afternoons. She was a thin, drab girl of sixteen or seventeen who wore plain cotton dresses and mail order shoes. Even though everyone in the *Journal* office appeared to know her by name, Mae, she rarely spoke to anyone. Once Aaron asked Homer Witt who she was.

Witt answered with a shrug. "Catton's daughter, they say."

Monday morning Aaron met the man. Catton was late. When he finally arrived, he came into Homer Witt's office without knocking and slumped into a chair opposite the desk. Witt introduced Aaron to him, but when Aaron crossed the room and extended his hand, Sam Catton only nodded. Aaron withdrew his right hand from midair, feeling a mixture of embarrassment and anger.

Homer Witt explained the new working arrangement. Catton accepted the instructions with a single nod of his head.

Aaron followed Sam Catton out of the office, but before leaving the building Catton ducked into Henry Daniels' office. In a few minutes he came out. Aaron followed him downstairs and out of the building. Outside, Catton stopped and faced Aaron. At close range Aaron smelled the man's whiskey-soured breath.

"I've got the word on you, Mills. You're Witt's pet. Anything you say in that office goes for gospel. Well, that doesn't wash with me. I've got work to do, and I won't have some refugee from the social register slowing me down. Get in my way, Mills, and I'll knock you on your ass."

All that week Aaron made a point of not getting in Sam Catton's way. Aaron followed him and watched him, but he gave Catton plenty of room and kept silent even when he had questions to ask.

Aaron learned that Sam Catton had a regular drinking routine, but not a regular news beat. Monday through Friday of that week Aaron trailed after Catton as he wandered into city police court, the city marshal's office, and the United States marshal's office in the Federal Building. Catton talked to clerks and deputies as well as the city marshal and U.S.

marshal stationed in Denver. Catton knew many men in law enforcement and seemed well accepted by them.

Catton generally took his noon meal and "libation" at the Slaughterhouse. The saloon was only a long gap between two brick buildings, covered with a roof and closed off at either end by plank walls with batwing doors. A bar ran the length of the Slaughterhouse, and light was provided by lanterns suspended overhead on wires. At noon two-for-a-quarter drinks and a variety of sandwiches were served, drawing crowds from the nearby railyards as well as men from downtown.

By noon of every day Sam Catton had developed several outlines of stories he had picked up in the morning rounds. Early in the afternoon he would wind up the day's interviews, then move down to Blake Street or Holiday Street. Aaron went into establishments and saw sights that he had only imagined in his boyhood. He saw real "painted ladies," drunks sleeping on sawdust-covered floors, fights between gamblers and miners or cowboys, and heard talk of morphine addiction among prostitutes, and a notorious Negro saloon that was allowed to exist only because the black vote had been delivered to the Democrats.

At one saloon or another, invariably with electric-powered nickelodeons playing in the background, Sam Catton would find an unoccupied poker table and finish writing the day's copy. Catton, Aaron observed, was known by nearly every bartender, gambler, and madam in Denver. And he seemed as well accepted by them as he was by Denver's lawmen.

Generally, by three o'clock every afternoon Catton

would have his copy written. At this hour his daughter would appear and take his stories back to the *Journal.*

Aaron usually left Sam Catton at that time of day and walked back to the *Journal* with Mae Catton. She was very shy. When Aaron tried to strike up a conversation by asking questions, she answered with a nod or a shake of her head or a brief reply.

Late in the week Aaron asked Mae, "How do you know where to find your father every afternoon? He seems to have no pattern."

"I ask around," Mae said. Then she added rather proudly, "Everybody knows Daddy."

Aaron's impression was that Mae was tied to her father as a child would be. She never questioned Sam Catton. She seemed eager to carry out his instructions.

Yet Aaron sensed another quality in Mae, too, a certain toughness. Perhaps being in this section of Denver every day had given her that quality. Aaron thought back over his own childhood and realized that not long ago he would have been envious of Mae. She roamed through streets and wandered in and out of establishments that Aaron had seen only from a carriage window. In those days Aaron was fascinated by what he saw because it was so different from anything he knew. This "low life," as his mother called it, held the sweet promise of the forbidden.

After one week with Sam Catton, Aaron had learned more about the "low life" than he wanted to know, and he had learned very little about crime reporting. On Saturday morning Aaron went into Homer Witt's office and explained the situation.

"I know why Sam Catton's the best crime reporter

in the city," Aaron said. "He knows the right people—on both sides of the law. But he's no teacher. We hardly exchanged a word all week. He tolerated me, that was all."

"I see," Witt said, nodding thoughtfully. "What you need is an assignment." He paused. "Let me think this over, Aaron. I'll talk to Daniels and get back to you the first of the week."

Monday morning Aaron sat at his desk writing an article about Denver's annual spring ball when Witt tapped on his door and came in.

"Aaron, how often does Sam go into the U.S. marshal's office?"

Aaron thought back over the week. "Once last week. He talked to the clerk for a while, then left me behind while he went into the marshal's office."

Homer Witt winced. "I see what you mean when you say Sam is no teacher." Witt sat on the corner of Aaron's desk. "Not many federal cases are of local interest, but every once in a while we miss a good story there. Sam pays more attention to the city marshal and the county sheriff. And rightly so, generally speaking. However, I want you to take the U.S. marshal and federal court as a part of your regular beat. See what you can dig up."

"I'll start tomorrow," Aaron said.

Aaron was eager to begin. He thought Sam Catton would be glad to be rid of him. Aaron was wrong.

Shortly before noon on Tuesday Catton stormed into Homer Witt's office. Aaron heard the commotion and came out of his office to see what was happening. Along with five other reporters, Aaron heard snatches of the argument that raged between the two men.

After an exchange of shouts, Witt bellowed, "I run this newspaper, Sam!"

"You don't run my beat!" Catton yelled back.

Aaron heard a great crash in the office. A long silence followed and then subdued voices carried through the transom above the door.

The door swung open. Catton came out. When he saw Aaron, he altered his course and walked straight to him, jamming an index finger into Aaron's chest.

"Don't think you can sneak around behind my back and get away with it, Mills. Stay out of my territory."

Aaron brushed Catton's hand away. "I'm not sneaking around anywhere."

"The hell," Catton said in a low, menacing voice. "You've been warned." He abruptly turned away and walked out of the office, casting a glaring look back at Homer Witt before passing through the door.

Aaron saw Henry Daniels. The city editor stood in his office doorway, smiling.

Witt stepped into his office and then came out, carrying a broken chair. "Sam has a temper," he said.

The remark was met by nervous laughter from the reporters in the outer office. Homer Witt turned and looked at Aaron.

"You keep that new assignment," he said. "If Sam gives you any trouble, let me know. We'll try to settle it peaceably."

Aaron said, "Catton told me once that if I ever got in his way, he'd knock me on my ass."

"Will you let him do that?" Witt asked.

"No, sir," Aaron said.

Witt grinned. "When I was about your age, my father told me that I should respect my elders until they proved they weren't deserving. Then it was up to me to face them, man to man. I believe that's still good advice."

In the afternoon Aaron rode a yellow trolley car to the Federal Building. A bespectacled clerk manned a small desk in the outer office. Aaron remembered him from the time he had been here with Sam Catton. The clerk was a slender man in his mid-thirties who slicked his thinning hair straight back against his skull.

Aaron introduced himself and asked to see the United States marshal.

The clerk glanced at Aaron, then went back to his work. He made notes on some kind of government forms. "Marshal Burns isn't seeing any reporters today."

"I'll make an appointment," Aaron said.

"Marshal Burns will be out of the office for the rest of the week," the clerk said without looking up.

Aaron looked down at the man's balding head. "How about next week?"

The clerk shrugged.

Aaron sensed this was no ordinary run-around. He remembered that Sam Catton had been welcomed by the clerk. They had exchanged jokes, then Sam had gone into the marshal's office. Catton must have come in here and asked the clerk to be unco-operative with the new reporter from the *Denver City Journal*. Ignore him and he'll go away, Catton must have said. Aaron felt the same sense of frustration and rage that he had experienced years ago when Mrs. Armbrister had prevented him from seeing Sadie Anne.

Aaron quickly stepped around the small desk. He grabbed the clerk's starched shirtfront and yanked him to his feet. The clerk's eyes bulged. He started to cry out, but Aaron twisted his shirt and choked off his voice.

"How long have you been taking orders from Sam Catton?" Aaron demanded.

The clerk choked. Aaron loosened his grip and let him speak. "Let . . . let go."

Aaron tightened his hold for several seconds, then loosened it.

The clerk said hoarsely, "I don't take orders from Catton."

Aaron grasped his shirtfront with both hands and lifted the clerk off the floor. "I want the truth out of you, mister. Sam Catton was here, wasn't he?"

The clerk, bug-eyed, nodded frantically.

Aaron let him down, but did not release him. "What did he tell you?"

"Catton said you're trying to take his work away from him," the clerk said.

"I'm not," Aaron said. He let the clerk go. "But I am covering this office for the *Journal*. You might as well get used to seeing me walk through that door."

The clerk nodded and slowly collapsed into his chair, rubbing his throat.

"When can I see Marshal Burns?" Aaron asked.

The clerk opened an appointment book. "This afternoon. Four o'clock."

"Thank you," Aaron said. He turned and left the office.

At four o'clock Aaron found Marshal Burns to be an overweight, red-faced man who looked more like a grocer than a lawman. Burns's job, Aaron learned, was largely clerical. He handled communications and co-ordinated regional assignments in the investigations of federal cases.

Burns was very co-operative. He gave Aaron a

lengthy rundown on the federal cases that were pending. Aaron took careful notes and returned to his office and wrote a thousand-word article based on the information Burns had given him. Aaron deposited the copy in the city editor's basket. Aaron believed this story would be of limited interest to Denverites, however, and he doubted the article would ever see print.

In the morning, when Aaron came to work, he was met by Homer Witt.

"Step into my office for a minute, Aaron."

Aaron crossed the outer office and entered Witt's office. Witt closed the door behind him.

"I read your story on pending federal cases," Witt said, sitting in the swivel chair behind his desk. "Fine job. Daniels didn't want to run it, but I overruled him. We'll cut it some and put it on the front page."

Aaron was surprised. "That's good news."

"Speaking of news," Witt said, "did you hear what happened to the Armbrister mansion last night?"

"No," Aaron said. "What?"

"Some of the interior walls were broken open with a sledgehammer," Witt said. "Someone was probably looking for a hidden safe. You've probably heard the stories about the fortune in gold that is supposedly hidden away in that place."

Aaron nodded, even though he was only dimly aware of such stories. He did not like to think about the Armbristers or their mansion. Aaron did know that the mansion had been bequeathed to the city of Denver, and the city fathers had never been able to figure out what to do with it. The mansion had been unoccupied since the death of Mrs. Harriet Armbrister.

"I have an idea for a serialized article," Witt said.

"This has been on my mind for some time. Perhaps the time is right now."

"On what subject?" Aaron asked.

"The Armbristers," Homer Witt said. "They were an important family in the history of this city. Even though Wallace and I were philosophically opposed on just about everything, I had a certain admiration for the man. He had an exceedingly strong personality and a kind of ruthless strength. I would like to run a long article not only on Wallace, but on the whole family. Perhaps the article could begin with the incident last night in the empty mansion, then go back to Wallace's early days in this area, how he struck it rich, and so on."

"Sounds like a good idea," Aaron said. "When will you start it?"

Witt grinned. "The question is, when will you start it?"

Chapter IX

Aaron shook his head in surprise. He felt an immediate sense of dread. "Sir, I don't think I—".

Homer Witt raised one hand and interrupted Aaron. "You are the right man for this job, Aaron. I'll wager you're the only journalist in the state who was on speaking terms with any of the Armbristers. I imagine you and your mother were guests of hers in that mansion more than once, weren't you?"

Aaron nodded.

Witt smiled. "You'll have a front page by-line for several weeks."

Aaron exhaled. Witt was making the job sound attractive and Aaron would have jumped at it had the subject been anything but the Armbristers. Yet he knew he had no choice. Witt was counting on him. Turn Witt down and Aaron's relationship with him would never be the same.

"All right," Aaron said. "I'll give it a try. But I may need some help."

"I'm prepared to give you plenty of help," Homer Witt said. "I've compiled some old newspaper clippings for you to read. I'll send a couple of books to your office that you can use as reference material." Witt stood. "Let that assignment in the U.S. marshal's office go for the time being. Get right on this

Armbrister project. Between that and your society page, you'll have your hands full."

Aaron left Homer Witt's office wondering if it was only coincidence that he was being pulled off the crime beat now. Perhaps Witt thought he was avoiding trouble this way.

Aaron began reading about the Armbrister family that afternoon. Despite his overwhelming sense of dread with the whole project, he did become engrossed in the life of Wallace Armbrister. Armbrister was a man who started with nothing and in the space of a year he attained one of the greatest gold fortunes in the state's history.

The location of Wallace Armbrister's gold strike was a willow-choked gulch in the foothills not far from Denver. In 1860 Clear Creek Canyon was filled with men panning gold and operating sluice boxes. Wallace Armbrister, always a loner, moved his sluice box out of the main canyon into a side gulch. At that time of year, fall, the gulch carried little more than a trickle of water. Alone in the gulch, Wallace Armbrister built a small dam, then used the stored water to wash sand in the streambed. After a week's labor, he had accumulated a handful of peanut-sized gold nuggets.

Wallace Armbrister moved upstream. He built another dam and within a week had found more nuggets. These were larger and more rough-edged than the others. Armbrister correctly judged that the source was not far away, because the tumbling action of a stream rounded the soft gold nuggets as they broke away from a vein.

Upstream half a mile, quite a distance away from the hundreds of gold seekers in Clear Creek Canyon, Wallace Armbrister used a pick and shovel to dig a hole in the bottom of the gulch that came to be named for him. He uncovered a vein of gold ore that was thicker than his boot. Underground it widened.

From that first discovery, Wallace Armbrister amassed his fortune. He bought other mines in the Colorado Rockies, and he bought many lots in Denver. Armbrister lost money on every mine he bought, but his city property investments proved to be lucrative in the next decade.

With wealth, Wallace Armbrister became flamboyant and monumentally rude. He cared little whom he offended, but he easily took offense at the behavior of others. In 1869, when he decided he had been slighted by a desk clerk in a Denver hotel, Wallace Armbrister purchased the hotel and personally fired the clerk. Six weeks later Armbrister lost the same hotel in a high stakes poker game.

In 1872 Wallace Armbrister rented an entire passenger train and carried two hundred citizens of the territory back to Washington, D.C., to plead for statehood. A unique petition was presented to the newly re-elected President Ulysses S. Grant. The territory, when granted the status of statehood, should be named after its wealthiest citizen—Wallace Armbrister.

Back in Denver Wallace Armbrister was asked why he did not run for mayor of the city. His reply became widely associated with the Armbrister name: "I already own one."

Aaron read of the extravagant entertaining that took place in the Armbrister mansion after its completion in 1873. Harriet Armbrister became known as "The Queen of the Queen City." Summer lawn parties lasted late into the nights under sparkling stars; in winter the mansion's colorful windows sparkled from within by gaslight when the ballroom was filled with merrymakers. One of the largest parties of all was the debutante ball held for Cleo Armbrister.

Aaron discovered that very little had been written of the suicide of Wallace Armbrister in May of 1875. In the newspaper clippings at hand, Aaron saw only brief mention of the event: Wallace Armbrister, the Colorado Gold Baron, had shot himself while staying in a room at the Western Hotel on Blake Street.

One article in the file from a newspaper that was no longer in existence stated that Wallace Armbrister was with a young woman at the time of his death. Aaron scanned the article and was about to move on to the next when a name caught his eye. The young woman was named Sadie Anne Coltrane.

For several moments Aaron was too stunned to think clearly. His eyes held to the name "Sadie Anne" as though magnetized.

Aaron's memory flashed back to the first time he saw Sadie Anne. That hot August afternoon of his sixteenth year was stamped into his memory. Even now Aaron could close his eyes and visualize Sadie Anne coming across the portico of the Armbrister mansion.

"Moose," she had joked when Aaron asked her name, "Moose Armtwister." Aaron remembered so vividly that he could almost hear her voice. Then she had said she wanted to be called "Sadie Anne." The name had been her mother's.

Aaron opened his eyes and looked down at the yellowed newspaper article on his desk. May 4, 1875, was the date of Wallace Armbrister's suicide. Seeing that date revealed a shocking truth to Aaron. He knew Sadie Anne's age. The time fit too well to be coincidence. Sadie Anne was the child of Sadie Anne Coltrane and Wallace Armbrister. Sixteen years later, living in the mansion of the man who had fathered her, the girl had taken her mother's name.

But why had Wallace Armbrister shot himself?

Aaron pondered the question in the back of his mind and at once tested his theory about Sadie Anne against what he knew. Aaron was certain he was right, even though he might never be able to prove it. Aaron recalled Mrs. Armbrister's reaction the first time he let the name "Sadie Anne" slip out. The old woman had flinched. "Don't call her by that name!" Mrs. Armbrister had shouted.

The last night Aaron saw Sadie Anne was memorable, too. She had made an obscure but disturbing remark about herself. "I know who I am. I can't escape myself."

Aaron wondered how long Sadie Anne had known her own identity. Had Mrs. Armbrister told her on the day that she failed to come to the summerhouse? Perhaps so. But Aaron still was at a loss to explain the presence of the white-haired man and the stocky young man he had seen in the drawing room.

Aaron felt frustrated by the fact that he could never prove his theory, and he could never learn all there was to know about Sadie Anne and the murder of Mrs. Armbrister. At least he could not find the whole truth by reading these old newspaper articles. All Aaron could see before him were tantalizing loose ends of a mysterious truth, a truth Sadie Anne must have known.

Where had she gone? The question that lurked

deep in Aaron's mind now came to the surface like a bubble of air released under water. When the bubble hit surface, Aaron saw . . . nothing.

Aaron came to understand the Armbrister chronicle in terms of extremes. Wallace and Harriet Armbrister and their young daughter Cleo had known the darkest side of poverty until Wallace's gold strike in 1860. From then on the family had enjoyed great wealth. But from then on, too, the life of the Armbrister family was marked by extreme tragedy: Wallace's suicide, the accidental death of Cleo, the murder of Harriet. And now Aaron was convinced he had uncovered the existence of an illegitimate child.

Aaron's thoughts were interrupted by a knock on his office door. Homer Witt opened the door and leaned in.

"All work and no play makes Aaron a dull boy," Witt said. "Everybody but you has gone home for the day."

"I didn't realize it was so late," Aaron said, leaning back in his chair and stretching.

"How are you coming with the Armbrister project?" Witt asked.

"I've got most of the reading done," Aaron said. "I'll start writing tomorrow."

"Good," Witt said.

"Wallace Armbrister was quite a man, wasn't he?" Aaron said.

"Yes, he was," Homer Witt said. "A mad genius, someone once called him."

"Did you know him?" Aaron asked.

"Only by sight," Witt said. "In those days I was just getting started in the newspaper business. I remember seeing his gold carriage on the streets a few times. People would stop and look when that carriage came along, as though a king had passed by. I imagine Wallace Armbrister liked to think of himself as a king hereabouts."

"I can't figure out why he shot himself," Aaron said.

"Neither could anyone else," Witt said.

"One newspaper article I read reported he was with a woman when he committed suicide," Aaron said.

Witt smiled. "He had many women."

"This one was named Sadie Anne Coltrane," Aaron said.

"Doesn't ring a bell with me," Witt said. He studied Aaron for a moment. "You think she might still be alive—and willing to talk?"

"It's possible," Aaron said.

"Interesting idea," Witt said, "very interesting. How do you propose to follow up on it?"

Aaron shrugged. "I don't know yet."

"Well, keep after it," Witt said.

Aaron left the *Journal* building with Witt. Outside they parted company. Aaron started to walk home, but suddenly changed his mind. He walked to a trolley stop and caught the next one to Armbrister Hill.

Aaron hopped off the trolley one block away from Maple Avenue. He walked through his old neighborhood, feeling a jumble of memories seep through him. He stopped in front of the house he had grown up in. The new owners had put a white picket fence around the yard and a new coat of white paint on the frame house. Aaron looked upstairs at his bedroom window. A shade was drawn against the setting sun.

Aaron turned away and strode down to the corner, turning on the street that led up Armbrister Hill. His breath grew short before he reached the top. He knew he had put on some weight over the winter, but until now he did not realize what poor condition he was in. He was sweating heavily by the time he reached the mansion drive. The iron gate between the stone lions was closed and bound with a heavy, rusting chain and a large padlock.

Aaron leaned against the gate and peered through the iron bars at the mansion. One of the huge stained glass windows was boarded over, perhaps a casualty of the break-in. The walk to the steps was weed-grown, and nearby shrubs grew with abandon.

On impulse, Aaron placed one hand on the gate's top crossbar and pulled himself up. He lifted one leg until he gained a foothold, and swung the other leg over. Aaron dropped to the ground on the other side.

He mounted the steps and walked across the portico to the front door. A notice was tacked on: *KEEP OUT By Order Of The City Marshal.*

Aaron walked to the far end of the portico, then back to the west end, where he had first met Sadie Anne. Aaron looked out to the west at the mountains beneath the evening sky. He recalled his thoughts when he had first seen this spectacular view. In the opposite direction, spectacular in its own way, was the great stretch of prairie.

In 1859 Wallace Armbrister had come across that prairie with thousands of other gold seekers. They had swarmed into the mountains, working feverishly in canyons and gulches. A few made wages until winter struck; many more left, disillusioned. Hundreds died from harsh weather and working in cold water day after day. Wallace Armbrister made a fortune.

Aaron now wondered if Armbrister had designed this mansion specifically to take advantage of this view. Aaron was quickly brought out of his thoughts when he heard a footfall behind him. He whirled to see a uniformed policeman standing on the portico, holding a long nightstick in his right hand.

"Don't move," he said as he slowly advanced.

Aaron glanced beyond the policeman and saw that the mansion door stood open several inches, much as it had when Sadie Anne had come through it.

"What are you doing here?" the policeman asked. He was a heavyset man with a pockmarked face, thick lips and round, sad eyes.

"I'm from the *Denver City Journal*," Aaron managed to say. "I'm on assignment. I understand burglars broke into the mansion yesterday."

"Got any identification?" the policeman asked.

Aaron reached into his coat pocket and brought out a card with his name printed beneath *Denver City Journal*.

The policeman looked at the card for a long minute, his lips moving as he read.

"Were you here when it happened?" Aaron asked.

The policeman's eyes shot to Aaron's. "Hell, no, I wasn't here. Don't write nothing about me. I was on duty across town."

"Who was on duty here?" Aaron asked.

"Nobody," he said.

"The mansion was unguarded?" Aaron asked.

"That's right," he said. "But it will be guarded from now on, what I hear."

"How much damage was done in there?" Aaron asked, pointing toward the door.

"A couple walls got knocked in," the policeman said. "Some door handles was stoled. They're gold-plated, you know."

"So I've heard," Aaron said. "You think the burglars found anything?"

"Naw, there ain't no treasure in there," he said.

"How do you know?" Aaron asked.

"After the old lady died," he said, "engineers from the city came up here and went all through the place. They had the original blueprints with them. They didn't find anything."

"Mind if I go in and look around?" Aaron asked.

The policeman shook his head. "Ain't nobody supposed to be in there who ain't authorized."

"I'll go see if I can get Marshal Greene to authorize me, then," Aaron said.

The policeman's face darkened for a moment. "You know Greene?"

"I've met him," Aaron said.

"Well, if you get his permission," the policeman said, "I'll give you the grand tour. I'll show you where the maid was murdered. There's still bloodstains in the carpets upstairs."

"I wouldn't want to miss that," Aaron said.

"I'll show you the whole place," he said. "You come back with being authorized, that's all I ask."

Aaron descended the steps and followed the walk to the drive. He scaled the gate and walked down the hill, past Maple Avenue, and on to the trolley line. Light was growing thin. Aaron felt tired from all the exercise of the last couple of hours. He looked at the clear sky. The weather was good now. He decided to start riding his Green Machine again.

At the boarding house Aaron found a letter from his mother. She wrote that Jennifer had given birth to a son. The name "we" chose, she said, was Jacob Oliver Hayes.

She concluded the letter by advising Aaron to marry and have children of his own. After all, as the man of the family he had the duty of propagating the Mills line. "You'll be much happier and your life will be fuller. You have a tendency toward solitude, Aaron, that causes me worry."

Aaron resented her presumptuous advice from nearly half a continent's distance. She seemed overly eager to remind him of his supposed duties. Beneath his resentment, though, the words in the letter struck a chord. Aaron was not happy, even though he was successful in his work. At the *Journal*, as in college, Aaron had not made a single friendship, save that of Homer Witt. Aaron's office isolated him from the other journalists. So did his position on the staff. The one reporter who worked the news beat for the society page treated Aaron distantly, as most employees would treat their boss.

Aaron felt satisfied with his success, but regretted not having anyone close to him to share it with. As Aaron lay in bed that night in the silent darkness of his boarding house room the image of Sadie Anne came into his mind. He realized he would never be happy, or able to form another close relationship, until he found Sadie Anne, or at least discovered what had happened to her.

Chapter X

One o'clock Tuesday afternoon Aaron rode his Green Machine downtown to the Denver Police Court Building. He rounded a corner in front of the three-story building and saw City Marshal Floyd Greene heading up the steps. Aaron hopped off his bicycle. He leaned it against the wall and ran up the steps and hailed the marshal.

At the top landing Greene stopped and looked back.

Aaron said breathlessly, "I'm Aaron Mills of the *Journal.*"

"Who set your tail afire?" Greene asked.

Aaron smiled. "I'm glad I caught you. I'm working on an assignment about the Armbrister family. I'd like to get into the mansion, but I'm told I have to have an authorization from you."

"That's right," Greene said. "Come up to my office and I'll give you one."

Aaron walked with him across the polished main floor of the building to the city marshal's office. A police clerk at a front desk responded to Greene's request by opening a bottom drawer and pulling out a blank form. Greene took a pen from a well on top of the desk and quickly scribbled in the necessary information.

"What's your name again?" Greene asked.

"Aaron Mills."

Greene wrote the name in, then handed the form to Aaron. "Just give this to the officer on duty." He paused. "Don't I know you?"

"I came in here with Sam Catton a while back," Aaron said.

"Now I remember," Greene said. "You were learning the tricks of the trade from an old hand."

"That was the idea," Aaron said.

"Sam's quite a fellow," Greene said, "quite a fellow. He's been writing crime news for a lot of years. Gets it straight, too—usually." Greene chuckled. "He plays a bad hand of poker, though."

Aaron left the office and walked across the lobby and out the main door. He descended the steps, unaware that someone followed him until he reached street level and heard his name spoken.

"Mills."

Aaron turned and saw Sam Catton.

"What are you doing here, Mills?"

It was not a question, but a challenge. Aaron debated whether to answer. He wanted to avoid trouble. After meeting Catton's glare for a minute, Aaron said, "I was talking to Marshal Greene."

"I know," Catton said through clenched teeth. "What about?"

"That doesn't concern you," Aaron said.

"Tell me, or take your punishment," Catton said.

"Punishment?" Aaron said. "For what?"

"I warned you once, Mills," Catton said.

Aaron was aware that a crowd had formed around them. He overheard someone say, "Get Greene."

Catton said, "Now, I'm through warning you. I'm going to teach you."

Catton moved a step closer and cocked his right

fist back. He swung, roundhouse style. Instinctively, Aaron's left arm shot up, blocking the punch. With his right, Aaron counter-punched. The short, powerful blow struck Catton on the jaw.

Sam Catton was rocked back. Aaron hit him again, with a left. Catton's eyes rolled. He sank to his knees and stumbled forward. Aaron caught him, keeping him from falling on his face.

Aaron became aware of shouts. He looked up and between the shoulders of two bystanders, he saw Marshal Greene bounding down the steps.

"What's going on here?" he demanded.

One of the bystanders, a full-bearded man who wore a derby, spoke up. "I saw what happened, Marshal. This young man was minding his own business when that feller came up and threatened him and swung on him."

"That's right," said another. "The youngster there defended himself. With two punches he dropped that man."

"Damn near took his head off," said a third man.

Greene knelt beside Sam Catton, who lay on the walk. Catton's eyes fluttered and his lips moved, but he seemed unable to speak. Greene looked up at Aaron.

"Why is Sam riled?"

Aaron said, "I guess he thinks I'm trying to take over his territory. He must have seen me talking to you."

"Hell, I thought you pen pushers were peaceful," Greene said.

"I didn't mean to hit him," Aaron said.

The full-bearded bystander laughed. "I'd hate to see what you'd do if you put your mind to it!"

Catton moaned and tried to sit up.

Greene said to Aaron, "Sam's hot-blooded. I reckon things would go easier here if you wasn't around when he comes to his senses."

Aaron turned and went to his bicycle. He rolled the machine out to the street and mounted. As he pedaled away, he looked back over his shoulder. Marshal Greene and one of the bystanders had helped Sam Catton to his feet. Catton's knees were obviously weak, but he held his head up.

Aaron had told the truth when he said he did not intend to hit Sam Catton. Aaron had not fought since he had been on the Hawkins Academy boxing team, but today he had punched Sam Catton purely on reflex. As he pedaled down the street and turned the corner on the avenue that eventually led to Armbrister Hill, Aaron was still amazed at himself.

He tried to pedal all the way up Armbrister Hill, but was able to go only half the distance. He dismounted and pushed the Green Machine to the mansion's gate. After resting a few minutes, he climbed over the iron gate.

The big policeman came out on the portico and met him. Aaron dug the signed authorization out of his pocket and handed it to the policeman. He studied the document, then grinned.

"Well, come on in."

Aaron followed him into the entryway and down the mansion's main hall. Although the interior was lighted only by indirect light from outside and a musty smell was in the air, Aaron was overcome by a strong sense of the past. The white-haired Harriet Armbrister might appear suddenly, demanding to know what business they had in her home. *Get out! Get out!* she would scream.

The floor near the arched doorway was covered with debris that crunched underfoot.

"This is where the wall was busted in," the policeman said, his voice echoing.

Aaron looked through a hole in the wall a dozen feet short of the arched doorway. The drawing room was on the other side of the wall.

The policeman pointed to a spot beyond the doorway. "Busted in down there, too."

Aaron moved to the doorway and entered the drawing room. Light filtered in through the stained glass windows. What once must have been a beautiful sight was now an eerie one. Colorful light from the windows shone upon a drawing room that was in ruin. The portraits had been pulled from the walls. Where they had hung, the walls were damaged. The carpet was torn and pulled up in several places.

Aaron walked to the fireplace. Wallace Armbrister's portrait leaned against the hearth. Aaron came closer and saw that it had been disfigured. Long, slashing cuts ran diagonally across the painted image.

"Now, why would anybody do a fool thing like that?" the policeman said. He stood behind Aaron, looking down at the ruined portrait. "Kids done it, if you ask me. I don't know what to think of kids anymore. They're hellions. All they can think about is wrecking property. They don't respect nothing, kids don't."

Aaron left the drawing room. He walked to the end of the hall to the service entrance and the back staircase. For a moment his eyes lingered on the spot at the base of the stairs where he had seen the body of Harriet Armbrister, but then he went to the door and looked outside. The summerhouse was still there. It needed paint. The door stood open. The surrounding grounds were shaggy with weeds.

Aaron walked down the hallway to the main entrance. The policeman came along behind, offering to take him upstairs.

"I've seen enough," Aaron said, stepping out onto the wide portico.

"Why, you ain't seen nothing of the upstairs," the policeman said. He paused. "Say, what was you looking for?"

"Nothing in particular," Aaron said. He turned and faced the policeman. "Do you happen to know a man named Ross Hogan?"

"Damned right, I do," he said. "Hogan was the best damned city marshal this town's ever seen. I broke into the force when he was running the show. He's my kind of lawman. He never hid behind no desk."

"Does Floyd Greene?" Aaron asked.

The policeman scowled. "I never said that. Don't you go writing in your paper that I said that." He added, "I got my opinions, that's all."

"Where is Hogan now?" Aaron asked.

The policeman turned and pointed to the mountains. "A year ago he and his boy was up there, working a mine."

"Do you know where?" Aaron asked.

"A gulch off Clear Creek Canyon," he said. "Let me think. Hogan came to town last year. Told me all about the place." He paused, brow lined with thought. "Sunrise Gulch. That's it. Sunrise Gulch. A couple miles up Sunrise Gulch. He said he had a cabin off on the left side of the road. Told me to come up and see him. I wanted to, but never got around to it."

"Thanks," Aaron said.

"You going to hunt him up?"

Aaron nodded.

"Well, say howdy for me," the policeman said.

"I will," Aaron said. He walked down the steps and had reached the gate before he realized he did not know the policeman's name. Aaron looked back and saw that the portico was empty. The door was slowly closing, leaving Aaron with an eerie feeling.

Aaron rode his machine down Armbrister Hill and across town toward the boarding house. On the way he took a familiar turn and wheeled past the red brick building that had once housed Mills Job Printers. The structure had been converted to a warehouse for a mining supply company. Aaron slowed, saw where his father's sign had been painted over, and then he rode on to the boarding house.

Events of the day had stirred countless memories in Aaron's mind. He remembered his father. One image in his mind was as clear as a photograph. He saw his father sitting at the rolltop desk in the front office of Mills Job Printers. Jacob Mills turned in his swivel chair, looked up at Aaron, and smiled.

Aaron saw irony in one fact. The great mansion atop Armbrister Hill was slipping into ruin while at the bottom of the hill the modest house that Aaron grew up in was freshly painted, and the owners thought enough of the wallpaper upstairs to pull the shade against the afternoon sun.

In the morning Aaron explained to Homer Witt why he wanted to interview Ross Hogan. Witt was skeptical about the plan and doubted that Aaron would learn much that was new in the Harriet Armbrister murder case.

"Maybe not," Aaron said, "but he might know of a woman named Sadie Anne Coltrane."

Witt smiled. "Now, there's an interesting notion. Let me know what you've found out when you get back."

Aaron rode his Green Machine downtown to the City Livery. He rented a one-horse buggy and got directions from the liveryman on how to drive to Clear Creek Canyon. The canyon was less than twenty miles away.

Once Aaron left Denver, he pushed the horse hard and reached the mouth of the canyon before noon. Clear Creek was the color of rust. Aaron stopped beside the stream and ate a lunch he had brought while the harnessed horse grazed nearby. The air that came on a mountain breeze was cool and smelled of pine.

Aaron followed the freight road up the canyon, past a noisy stamp mill where ore was crushed, and a collection of shacks and cabins. Aaron saw a few miners farther up the canyon. They wore overalls and knee-high boots splattered with mud. From one of them he received directions to Sunrise Gulch and the Hogan cabin.

Sunrise Gulch was marked by a crude sign on a stake beside the road. The gulch was a narrow, steep-sided rift between two mountains. The mountainsides were covered with pine trees, growing as thick as hair on a hide.

The road that ran up the gulch was little more than two deep ruts ground into the rocky earth by the heavy wheels of ore wagons. Streams of water ran down both ruts, either from melting snow in the high country or a spring cut by a mine tunnel somewhere ahead.

Most of the mines were high on the mountainside. Where pine trees had been cut away Aaron saw yellowed mounds of rock and soil that had been carried out of the earth.

He might have driven past the cabin if he had not been watching for it. The pine forest, down by the creek, was broken by a patch of aspen trees. Deep in the shadows of this grove was a low cabin. Aaron turned off the road. The windowless cabin was built entirely of pine logs, even the roof.

Aaron drove the buggy across a creek and followed a path through the white-barked aspen trees, whose leaves clattered with a breeze. Branches slapped at the buggy. As Aaron drew near the cabin, he heard a baby crying. He stopped the buggy by the front door.

"Hello!" he called.

The baby stopped crying. A young woman opened the door and peeked outside. She held her baby in the crook of one arm.

"Yes?" she asked.

"I'm Aaron Mills. I came out from Denver to see Ross Hogan. Is this his place?"

The young woman hesitated. "Yes."

"Is he here?" Aaron asked.

"He . . . he's up at the mine," she said.

"Where is it?" Aaron asked.

"They don't want strangers up there," she said.

"Mind if I wait a while?" Aaron asked. "It's important that I see him."

The woman ducked back into the cabin and closed the door.

Aaron got out of the buggy. He walked to one side

of the cabin, then back to the other. A trail ran through the aspen grove, angling up into the pine forest. Aaron guessed that trail led to Ross Hogan's mine. He was debating whether to follow it when a small, hard object jabbed into his back.

"Get your hands up. Real slow."

Aaron was startled, but did as he was told. He felt the man behind him pull up his light coat.

"I'm not armed," Aaron said.

"Turn around. Slow, real slow."

Aaron turned and saw an aged Ross Hogan. His face was deeply lined and his gray hair had thinned, but he still wore a full mustache. Hogan held a revolver in his hand, aimed at Aaron's chest.

"I don't know you," Hogan said.

"We only met once," Aaron said, "when you investigated the murder of Mrs. Harriet Armbrister and three of her maids."

Lines in Hogan's face deepened, then his eyes brightened with recognition. He smiled. Aaron realized then what had changed his appearance most: He had no teeth.

"Why, sure, I remember you. What's your name again?"

"Aaron Mills."

"Mills," Hogan said. "Sure, I remember you." He looked down at the revolver in his hand as though just then discovering it. He quickly lowered the weapon and thrust it into his belt. "I'm sorry for throwing down on you like that, Mills. I got to be careful, an old lawman like me. More than one yahoo has threatened to plant me over the years."

"I understand," Aaron said.

"What did you want to talk over?" Hogan asked. He glanced back at the cabin as he spoke. The young woman stood in the open doorway cradling not an infant but a carbine in her arms. Hogan waved to her. "It's all right, Susie." She stepped back into the darkness of the cabin and closed the door.

"I'd invite you inside," Hogan said, "but my grandson's teething. Squalls most of the day and night, seems like. I'd forgotten what trouble and pain there is in growing."

Aaron said, "I'm writing a story for the *Denver City Journal* about the Armbrister family. My curiosity has been stirred up all over again about the murder of Mrs. Harriet Armbrister. I want to ask you what happened to the investigation."

"Greene shelved it, that's what," Ross Hogan said, his voice rising in anger. "That case was my last one, turned out. I had just got started with the investigation when some drunk blowed a hole in my leg. While I was laid up in bed, the city retired me. The whole investigation got shelved."

"Did you pick up any clues as to the murderer's identity?" Aaron asked.

Hogan shook his head grimly. "Didn't have time. I figured the key to the whole case was that adopted daughter of old lady Armbrister's. Find out what happened to her, and you've got the answer in your pocket."

"Why do you say that?" Aaron asked.

Hogan squinted as though peering back into his memory. "The main thing is that the wall safe had been opened by the combination. The maid who survived because she was out of the mansion that night told me that the adopted daughter knew the combination."

"Maybe Mrs. Armbrister had been forced to open it," Aaron said.

"That's possible," Hogan admitted, "but we also found that some of the girl's clothes were gone. Now, if she had been taken by force, why would she pack a piece of luggage?" Hogan paused. "Say, I remember now. I called you in because the surviving maid told me you was meeting that girl every night out in the summerhouse."

Aaron nodded, but said nothing.

Suspicion crossed Hogan's face. "Did she come to see you after the murders?"

"No," Aaron said.

"You ever hear from her at all?" Hogan asked.

Aaron shook his head. "I wish I had. I think she's innocent."

"What gives you that idea?" Hogan asked.

Aaron shrugged. "Nothing I can point to."

"Well, the evidence points to her having some part in it," Hogan said. "I ain't saying she's a murderer, but I'd bet she knew who did it." He looked at Aaron for a moment. "And I'd bet something else."

"What?"

"Whoever murdered those women wouldn't leave any witnesses," Hogan said.

"I hope you're wrong," Aaron said.

"You aim to hunt for her?" Hogan asked.

"I will if I can come up with any leads," Aaron said.

"She was adopted," Hogan said. "Maybe you can find some paperwork on her somewhere."

"I'd sure like to know where," Aaron said.

"You didn't know her *that* well, huh?" Hogan asked with a toothless grin.

High on the mountainside Aaron heard a muffled explosion. Hogan turned around and looked up in that direction.

"My boy's shooting today," he said. "We're off the vein, but I got a feeling we're getting close. You know, when I think back over my life, I wonder if I shouldn't have mined instead of walking around Denver, making a target of myself. I gave the city of Denver thirty years of my life. What have I got to show for it? A certificate from the mayor and a bum leg. Well, maybe me and my boy will hit it big like crazy Wallace Armbrister did."

"Where is his mine from here?" Aaron asked.

"The Armbrister Mine?" Hogan asked. "Armbrister Gulch is about five miles fu'ther up the canyon. Runs parallel to Sunrise Gulch. But that gold country up there is played out. Has been for years. Nobody mines there anymore." He pointed up the mountainside. "Right here is where the next big gold strike is going to come. Mark my words."

"Good luck," Aaron said.

Hogan nodded. "Well, I hope you have some luck in tracing that girl."

Aaron walked to the buggy. Before climbing in, he asked Hogan, "Does the name Coltrane mean anything to you?"

Hogan shook his head slowly.

"Sadie Anne Coltrane?" Aaron asked.

"No, it don't," Ross Hogan said. "Why?"

"She was the mistress of Wallace Armbrister," Aaron said. "I've been wondering whatever happened to her."

"Why are you asking?" Hogan asked.

"In writing this story about the Armbristers," Aaron said, "I've wondered why Wallace shot himself. He had everything to live for. Sadie Anne Coltrane was with him in the Western Hotel when he blew his brains out."

"I was a deputy then," Hogan said. "I didn't handle the case. You think there's a tie-up between that suicide and the killings in the mansion?"

"I don't know," Aaron said. "I wish I did know."

"Mills, if you dig up any evidence in those murders, I'd like to know about it. I never did feel right about leaving that case up in the air. Hell of a way to end my career, if you get my meaning." Hogan paused. "I tried to get Greene to go after that investigation, but he kept telling me there wasn't enough evidence. Hell, you got to dig to find evidence. He wasn't willing to dig. Maybe you are."

"I will if I can find a starting place," Aaron said. He shook hands with Ross Hogan, thanked him for his time, and got into the buggy.

"Well, you let me know if you find anything," Hogan said again.

"I will," Aaron said.

Aaron turned the buggy and drove through the aspen grove to the road on the other side of the stream. He had learned little from Ross Hogan. And he had to admit that the evidence against Sadie Anne was strong.

Aaron reached Denver early in the evening. He felt tired and very hungry. He turned in the horse and buggy at the livery, then rode his Green Machine to a cafe and ate a late supper. By the time he got back to the boarding house, all he could think about was falling into bed. But he had company. Mae Catton sat on the floor outside his door.

Chapter XI

Mae got to her feet when she saw Aaron come into the hallway. She watched him approach, then threw a question at him like a stone.

"Why did you hit my father?"

"Ask him," Aaron said. He moved past her and unlocked his door. He entered his room and lit a lamp on the wall.

Mae stood in the doorway and called after him, "I'm asking you, Aaron Mills."

Aaron was too tired to have much patience. He ignored her. He took off his coat and tossed it on the bed. He sat on a chair at the foot of the bed and pulled off his boots.

"I want an answer!" Mae shouted.

Aaron felt a rush of anger. He almost shouted back at her. But he looked up and saw her standing in the doorway, hands on her small hips, leaning toward him. Her brown hair was tied in pigtails that bounced girlishly with the slightest move of her head, and her face, now pulled taut with anger, had never seen make-up, Aaron suspected. Mae was still a girl, but she was possessed with womanly outrage.

Aaron did not shout at her. "Well, don't stand out there yelling at me. Come in here. I'll tell you what happened."

Suddenly Mae grew shy and apprehensive. "I . . . I oughtn't be in your room . . . alone."

"Afraid of me?" Aaron asked lightly. He stood and walked to the oak washstand along one wall. He lifted the pitcher on top and poured water into a tin basin. Aaron washed his face, blindly grabbed a towel from the rack, and vigorously dried.

Aaron tossed the towel in the direction of the towel rack and crossed the room to the door. Mae stood there, head bowed.

"I'm sorry, Mae," Aaron said. "You caught me at a bad time."

Mae did not raise her head.

"I didn't want to fight with your father," Aaron said.

Mae said in a low voice, "I don't know what to do."

"What's wrong?" Aaron asked.

"Daddy's drunk," she said, "mean drunk. He says he wants to kill you." She raised her head and looked at Aaron. "He doesn't mean it, though. He's just drunk. He gets that way when everything's going bad. All I could think to do was come here and find out what happened."

"Mae, I don't have any quarrel with your father," Aaron said. "I've tried to stay clear of him."

"Daddy says you're trying to take his work away from him," Mae said.

"I'm not," Aaron said.

"But he saw you with Marshal Greene," she said.

"I had to talk to him," Aaron said. "I needed an authorization to get into the Armbrister mansion. If Sam had asked Greene, he'd have found that out."

Mae said, "Daddy's afraid of you."

"Afraid of me," Aaron said in surprise. "Why?"

"Because Mr. Witt is training you to take over Daddy's job," Mae said.

"That isn't true," Aaron said. "Homer Witt thinks your father is the best crime writer in Denver—in the whole state. He's not about to replace your father with me or anyone else."

For a moment Mae's face brightened. "Daddy should hear that. Will you tell him?"

"Mae, I don't think your father wants to see me—-"

"I don't mean tonight," Mae said quickly. "Tomorrow. Or day after. Come to our house and tell him what you just told me."

Aaron shook his head. "Mae, I can't do that. You should ask Homer Witt to talk to your father."

Mae looked down at the floor and nodded glumly. She moved out of the doorway into the hall.

"Mae—"

She turned and walked down the hall. Aaron called after her again, but she did not look back.

Aaron stepped back into his room and closed the door. He wondered if he had done the right thing. He could have agreed to talk to Sam Catton, but why should he? Aaron was the one who had been wronged.

Still, Aaron felt annoyed with himself. Mae apparently had her hands full with her father. Aaron's initial impression of her had not been accurate. He had thought Mae was childishly dependent on her father. Now he suspected that Sam Catton was in many ways dependent on his daughter.

In the morning Aaron was met in the empty outer office by Homer Witt.

"I understand you had a disagreement with Sam," Witt said.

"That's right," Aaron said. "How did you hear about it?"

"From Daniels, of course," Witt replied.

Aaron thought he detected a note of irritation in Witt's voice.

"I went to Marshal Greene's office and got the full story," Witt went on. "Greene says you knocked Sam silly with two punches. I didn't know you were a fighter."

"I didn't, either," Aaron said.

"Now, that sounds like false modesty," Witt said, grinning.

"I was on the Hawkins Academy boxing team," Aaron said. "But that was a long time ago."

"Sam got just what he deserved, according to Greene," Witt said. "For that reason, I won't follow up on the recommendation that Daniels made."

"What was that?" Aaron asked.

"That you be fired," Witt said.

"Fired," Aaron repeated.

Witt nodded. "Daniels thinks you riled Sam on purpose. Daniels told me that you know Sam's beat, and you arranged things so Sam would see you talking to Marshal Greene."

Aaron shook his head in disbelief. "Sam doesn't have a regular news beat."

Witt raised his hand. "I know. You don't have to defend yourself. Daniels is out of line. I have both sides of the story now. I'll reprimand Daniels first thing this morning." Witt added, "Sam missed a deadline. He knows I don't tolerate that. I've got a newspaper to run—with him, or without him."

Aaron was surprised to hear Witt say that.

"Sam's going to have to prove to me that he can keep off the bottle and on the job," Witt said. "If he doesn't, you'll be in line for his position. Could you handle it?"

"I'd hate to come into the job that way," Aaron said.

"As I said," Witt said, "I have a newspaper to run. I suspect Sam has missed deadlines before, but Daniels has covered up for him by rewriting old copy and running it. They're cozy. Well, this newspaper can run without either one of them." Witt added, "This is all between you and me, you understand."

Aaron nodded, but he felt very uncomfortable.

Witt changed the subject. "What did Ross Hogan have to say?"

Aaron gave a brief account of yesterday's conversation with the old lawman.

"I had a feeling he couldn't tell you much," Witt said. "I'd forgotten he wasn't city marshal when Wallace Armbrister committed suicide. When will you start writing the Armbrister story?"

"Today." Aaron said.

"Can I see Part One by Wednesday?" Witt asked.

"Yes," Aaron said, "I should have it done by then."

Witt nodded and grinned. "You're a hard worker, Aaron. I would guess your father is responsible for that trait in you. Show me a good man, and I'll point to a good father behind that man."

Aaron thanked him for the compliment. But after returning to his own office, Aaron felt strangely depressed and lonely. Witt's praise, instead of elating Aaron, weighed on him. Aaron needed someone to talk to, someone to confide in. He needed a friend, but had none.

Aaron mechanically wrote the society news for the next issue of the *Journal*, but he struggled with the writing of Part One of the Armbrister story.

Aaron began by writing a lengthy description of the mansion. He drew the account partly from his own memory, partly from descriptions of the mansion's construction that he had read in the reference material provided by Homer Witt. The writing brought back memories that Aaron had long suppressed, and by Wednesday, when Aaron turned the copy in, he felt emotionally wrung out.

"The story seems incomplete to me," Aaron said to Homer Witt. "My research has raised more questions than answers."

"Questions about why Wallace shot himself?" Witt asked. "And who murdered Mrs. Armbrister?"

Aaron nodded.

Witt smiled. "Those questions might never be answered."

"Did you know that whoever broke into the mansion slashed the portrait of Wallace Armbrister?" Aaron asked.

Witt's smile faded. "No, I didn't. What do you make of it?"

Aaron shrugged. "Another question."

"Are you on to something?" Witt asked.

"I don't have enough pieces of the puzzle to make a picture," Aaron said. "I have fragments of a picture, that's all. I wish I could find someone who knew more."

"Someone who's been around this town for a long time," Witt suggested, "and someone who kept his eyes and ears open."

Aaron nodded absently.

"I know someone who might be able to help you," Witt said.

Aaron looked at the editor-in-chief. His eyebrows bobbed when he spoke again.

"So do you."

Aaron asked, "Who?"

"Sam Catton," Witt said. "He's been a crime re-porter in Denver for a long time. Chances are he covered the Armbrister murder for the *Rocky Mountain News*."

With a shock Aaron realized Catton might have been one of the journalists he had seen in the front hallway of the mansion early that morning when the policeman had led Aaron to the end of the hall and to the corpse of Mrs. Armbrister. Aaron tried to visualize the journalists, but could not. He remembered their shouted questions, but not their faces.

"Do you want the answers to your questions badly enough to talk to Sam?" Witt asked.

"Yes, I do," Aaron said, "but I doubt that he'll talk to me."

"You never know," Witt said. "It's hard to figure what another man's thinking. Maybe every time Sam looks at you, he sees himself."

"What do you mean?" Aaron asked.

"I'd bet Sam Catton was not too different from you when he was a young man, just starting out," Witt said. "He was probably the most dedicated and hard-working journalist in town. Now he's gotten a hard edge on him and he's taken to drinking and gambling to excess. Maybe you remind him of bet-ter times—or of what could have been."

"I hadn't thought of it that way," Aaron said.

"I'm just speculating," Witt said. "Hard to know what's in a man's past, and what his private thoughts are." Witt paused and added, "But you might ask Sam for an interview."

For the remainder of the week Homer Witt's sug-gestion lurked in the back of Aaron's mind. He saw little chance of patching up his differences with Catton, yet he did want to talk to the man. An interview might be the right way to approach him. Aaron was convinced of one thing: Sam Catton was a journalist who knew more about local crimes and the people involved in them than the police.

Monday afternoon Aaron intercepted Mae after she delivered her father's copy to Daniels' basket. Mae tried to ignore Aaron. She walked down the staircase and out of the building with Aaron trailing after her.

"Mae," he said. "Mae." He reached out and grasped her arm.

Mae wrenched her arm away, throwing an angry glance back at him. "Leave me alone."

Aaron caught up with her and strode beside her on the boardwalk. "Mae, listen to me."

She cast another glance at him. "I don't need you."

Aaron almost said, *No, but I need you.* Instead he said, "I want to talk to Sam. It's important."

Mae slowed her pace, then stopped and faced him. "What's important?"

"Mae, I was wrong the other night—"

She interrupted, "No, you weren't. I shouldn't have asked you. Even if you told that to Daddy, he wouldn't have believed you."

"I let you down," Aaron said. "I'm sorry. But I do want to talk to your father. Do you think he'll see me?"

Mae looked at him searchingly. "I don't understand you, Aaron Mills. Sometimes you act so high and mighty."

"I don't mean to," Aaron said.

Mae said slowly, "No, you probably don't."

"Will you take me to your father?" Aaron asked.

Mae nodded. "All right. He's home now." She added, "Daddy's quit drinking."

Aaron and Mae caught a trolley that ran to Union Station, then walked along a narrow street that paralleled the rail-yards. The rutted street was lined with small frame houses. None had seen paint recently. Several had boarded windows and were surrounded with litter.

One house at the end of the block was tidier than the others. The one-story house caught Aaron's eye for that reason and because a man sat on a rocker on the porch. He was Sam Catton.

Catton watched them coming, then stood and went into the house. Mae glanced at Aaron, but said nothing until they reached the porch.

"Wait here," she said. "I'll go in and talk to him." Mae entered the house, closing the door behind her.

Several minutes passed before the door opened again. Mae leaned out. "Come in, Aaron."

Aaron walked into a small, sparsely furnished living room with a bare plank floor. A black, coal-burning heater stood in one corner. Wallpaper on the far wall was water-stained. Aaron read a framed motto over a pine bench: A Merry Heart Maketh A Cheerful Countenance. Sam Catton stood in the middle of the room. After looking at Aaron for a moment, he turned his attention to Mae.

"Leave us alone now, Mae."

She shook her head once. "I'm staying, Daddy." She motioned to a chair near the pine bench. "Aaron, sit down."

Aaron sat down and watched Mae cross the room. She brought a chair over for her father, then sat on the bench. Catton watched her in silence. He sat down and said to Aaron, "Women get hard to handle after they turn eighteen."

For a moment, Aaron was distracted. He had no idea Mae was eighteen years old. He looked at her until she blushed. Sam Catton shifted his weight, making the chair creak. Aaron came to.

Aaron said, "Sam, I didn't want to fight with you."

"I reckon I didn't give you much choice," he said, meeting Aaron's eyes.

"I don't have any notion of taking over the *Journal's* crime beat," Aaron said.

Catton nodded. "I should have known that. Hell, I shouldn't have raised my hand against you, Mills. Damned fool thing to do, letting my temper get away with me."

Aaron felt a great sense of relief. Sober, Sam Catton was a reasonable man. "I came here to ask you about a story you might have covered several years ago—the murder of Mrs. Harriet Armbrister."

"I covered it for the *News*," Catton said. "Axe murders. Three maids were killed, too."

"Any theories as to who did it?" Aaron asked.

"No," Catton said, studying Aaron. "Why?"

"This long article I've been writing about the Armbrister family has aroused my curiosity about several things. Those murders in the mansion is one."

Sam Catton ran a hand through his bushy hair, leaving strands of it falling to one side, over an ear. "Those murders were the most brutal I've ever seen. Whoever did it was crazy." He thought a moment. "I recall some theories that the old lady's adopted daughter might have had something to do with the murders. But that was only talk. There was no proof. Personally, I believe the girl was abducted and killed later."

For an instant Aaron considered asking Catton if he was one of the journalists in the front hall that morning, but quickly discarded the idea. Aaron was not prepared to lie to Sam Catton, but neither did he want to reveal all that he knew.

"Another question that's been on my mind," Aaron said, "is about Wallace Armbrister's suicide."

"That one had everybody wondering," Catton said.

"You remember it?" Aaron asked.

"Sure, I do," he said. He looked away from Aaron. "I was a young reporter for the *News* then—about your age, I suppose."

"Does the name Sadie Anne Coltrane mean anything to you?" Aaron asked.

Catton's head jerked around as he fixed his eyes on Aaron. "Coltrane. I haven't heard that name in a long time. A hell of a long time."

"What do you know about her?" Aaron asked.

Sam Catton smiled faintly. "You're interrogating me, Mills. I've got a strong feeling you're not putting all of your cards on the table."

"I don't have enough cards to play the game," Aaron said. "I came across the name of Sadie Anne Coltrane when I researched the Armbrister story. She was Wallace Armbrister's mistress, wasn't she?"

"One of them," Catton said. "Wait a minute. You think she might have some connection with the murder of Mrs. Armbrister?"

"The idea occurred to me," Aaron said.

"You're wrong on that one," Catton said. "Sadie Anne Coltrane's dead. She died about a year after Armbrister's suicide."

"She died here in Denver?" Aaron asked.

Catton nodded. "In the Western Hotel, as I remember. The old Western was a brothel, you know. Sadie

Anne poisoned herself—or took too much morphine. I've forgotten the details. She left a note saying what should be done with her children."

"How many did she have?" Aaron asked.

"Two," Catton said. "A boy and a girl. The boy was the oldest. I think he was four or five years old."

"She had them both by Wallace Armbrister?" Aaron asked.

"That was the talk," Catton said. "I reckon she's the only one who knew for sure, though." Catton paused. "I just remembered something else. Wallace Armbrister threatened to kill the children not long before he blew his brains out."

Mae gasped. "Kill his children!"

Catton looked at his daughter. "He was a madman, Mae. He left more than one ruined life behind him."

"What happened to the children?" Aaron asked.

"I was just trying to remember," Catton said slowly. "Seems like Sadie Anne's father came and got them. He took them home."

Aaron edged forward in the chair. "Where?"

Catton shrugged. "I don't remember."

"You must remember," Aaron said.

"I can't," Catton said, turning both hands palms up. "Maybe I never knew."

"Tell me!" Aaron said.

"Aaron, stop shouting!" Mae exclaimed.

Chapter XII

"I see you've got a temper, too," Sam Catton said.

"I'm sorry," Aaron said quickly. He stood. Sweat had broken out of his skin. For a moment he had believed a clue to a truth he had sought for many years was within his grasp.

"I'll do some inquiring, Mills," Catton said. "Maybe someone will remember where old man Coltrane came from."

Aaron thanked him and apologized again. He was aware that Mae stared at him.

Sam Catton chuckled and got to his feet. "At least we didn't come to blows this time, Mills."

"I hope we never do again," Aaron said, holding his hand out to shake. He well remembered that the first time he had tried to shake hands with Sam Catton his hand had been left hanging in midair.

Now Catton reached out and grasped Aaron's hand. "I share that hope. Last time you rattled my brain proper."

Aaron smiled. He liked Sam Catton's self-deprecatory manner. Aaron said good-by and walked to the door. Mae moved in front of him. She opened the door and stepped out on the porch with him.

"You've made me happy," she said. "I think I might be happier than you are."

Aaron was caught off guard by the blunt remark.

"Why do you say that?"

She looked at him a while before answering. "Just a feeling I have."

Aaron walked back to Union Station and caught a trolley. He was troubled by Mae's parting remark. Had she really seen through him so clearly? Aaron realized that in his anger a few minutes ago he had revealed something about himself. He felt uncomfortable. For some reason he found himself hoping that he would not see Mae again soon.

But Aaron saw her the following Thursday night. He answered a knock on his door and found her standing in the hallway of the boarding house.

"Mae?" Aaron said in surprise.

She smiled at him. Somehow she had transformed herself from a pig-tailed girl to a woman. She wore a long dress with a high collar. The puffed sleeves and hem were ringed with delicate lace. Mae's hair was long and soft now, and her cheeks and lips were rosy.

Mae laughed. "I wish you could see the look on your face."

"You look . . . older," Aaron said.

"If that's a compliment, I'll take it," she said.

Aaron felt his face grow warm. "I meant it as a compliment. You're beautiful, Mae." For a moment he saw a girlish shyness cross her face, but she held her head up and looked into his eyes.

Aaron asked, "Will you come in?"

She nodded. As she entered the room, Aaron saw that she walked differently. She moved like a woman. Aaron got a chair for her.

"Daddy decided I should start looking like a lady," Mae said, smoothing the lap of her dress. "I guess I like the idea."

"I do," Aaron said.

Mae laughed again. Then she said, "I've come to tell you what Daddy found out about the Coltranes."

Aaron sat on the edge of the unmade bed and listened to her.

"Sadie Anne Coltrane's father was named Luke," Mae said. "He owned a road ranch in eastern Colorado, on Straight Road. As far as Daddy could find out, Luke Coltrane took the body of his daughter and his two grandchildren back there."

"Does he still live there?" Aaron asked.

"Daddy couldn't find anyone who knew," Mae said.

"How far away from here is the Coltrane road ranch?" Aaron asked.

"One man Daddy talked to thought it was about fifty miles away," Mae said. "It was a popular stopping place before the railroad went through." She asked, "Have you ever been on Straight Road?"

Aaron shook his head. He had heard of the road. The name came from the fact that it ran almost straight across the prairie, connecting Denver with Kansas City. For many years the road had been an important freight artery.

"Will you try to find the road ranch?" Mae asked.

Aaron nodded absently. He was already thinking ahead, wondering when he could go.

"Why?" Mae asked. "What is the real reason you want to find the Coltranes?"

Aaron almost told her that it was only because of the Armbrister story, but stopped himself.

Mae said, "Sometimes it is good to talk to someone, Aaron. I'm a good listener. I won't repeat anything you tell me."

"The story is long and complicated," Aaron said. "I've never told anyone before." He stood and walked across the room. He thought he would not tell her, but when he turned and faced her, he saw a lovely woman seated in the chair, one he could trust.

When Aaron finished, he felt emotionally exhausted. Mae had listened intently, without saying a word. Aaron walked back to the bed and slumped down on it.

"Aaron, I . . ." Mae's voice was thick with emotion. "I understand." After a moment she added, "You're searching for Sadie Anne, but you may find a murderer."

"She's no murderer," Aaron said, too sharply.

"When will you leave?" Mae asked.

"As soon as I can get a few days off," Aaron said, sitting up on the bed. "I haven't had a vacation since I started working on the *Journal*. It's time I took one." But Aaron knew Homer Witt would object to his leaving now. Witt expected him to finish the Armbrister story. Besides, the search for the road ranch on Straight Road might well be a futile one.

Mae stood. "Aaron, if there is anything I can do to help you, please tell me."

"You already have," Aaron said. "You've given me the first solid clue."

They stood looking at one another for a long moment, then Mae turned and moved to the door.

"I'll walk you to the trolley," Aaron said.

The next day Aaron finished the second segment of the Armbrister story. He wrote of Wallace Armbrister's investments in mining and city property in Denver. Armbrister was a great believer in Denver's future, even though in those days much serious talk was circulating about moving the state's capital to one of the booming mining regions in the Rocky Mountains.

Aaron also wrote of life in the Armbrister mansion in those years. On the face of it, the times must have been happy ones for the Armbrister family. But Aaron wondered. The public face and the private face of the Armbristers must have been quite different.

On Saturday Aaron went into Homer Witt's office and requested three days of vacation. He explained that Sam Catton had provided him with a lead that should be followed up.

"Then I was right that Sam might prove helpful to you," Witt said. "But why are you taking your own time to go after this lead?"

"It's a long shot," Aaron said. "If I were just a reporter following a story, I probably would not bother with it."

"That's a pleasantly mysterious reason," Witt said. "The question is, when will you finish the business at hand?"

"I'll come into the office tomorrow and write the final part of the Armbrister article," Aaron said. "I'll leave it on my desk. You can pick it up Monday morning."

Witt nodded. "All right. Take your three days. Good luck to you."

Early Sunday morning Aaron rode his Green Machine through the empty streets of Denver to the *Journal* building. Coming to work at this time left Aaron with an eerie feeling, as though life on earth had stopped and he was the only man left, still going through the motions of his existence.

He wrote an account of the last days of Harriet

Armbrister and the murder scene at the mansion. Aaron completed the article by noon, but as he leaned back in his swivel chair and rubbed his eyes, he sensed that the real story, and perhaps a larger one, had not yet been revealed.

Aaron left the *Journal* and rode his machine downtown to the City Livery. He rented the same horse and buggy that he had used to go to Ross Hogan's cabin. This time Aaron took a feed bag and a three-day supply of oats.

He drove the buggy back to the boarding house. He planned to pack up the supplies and food he would need, and leave Denver early in the morning. When he entered the hallway that led to his room, he saw a small bundle on the floor by his door. A note was attached.

Aaron,
  My father once said that the pen is mightier than the sword, but sometimes a sword is needed to keep the pen alive. Be careful.

Mae

Aaron opened the cloth bundle. Inside was a small .32 caliber revolver in a shoulder holster, along with a box of ammunition. He pulled the revolver out of its holster. The weapon was scarcely larger than his hand. The name engraved on the butt was Samuel Catton.

Aaron unlocked his door and went into his room. His first thought was that he did not need a gun. But out of curiosity he took off his light coat and tried on the shoulder holster. It fit comfortably. The little revolver, like a deadly toy, rode snugly against his side. Aaron put on his coat and stood in front of the mirror on the washstand. The revolver was barely noticeable.

He took off the shoulder holster and hung it from the bed post. He packed the clothes he would need, and a box of canned food, cheese and crackers, and a canteen.

At dawn Aaron left the boarding house. He drove out of Denver on a main street that led to Straight Road on the eastern outskirts of the city.

Ahead the horizon grew light and turned pink, steadily brightening, then the hot, red ball of the sun came up. Aaron sat as far back in the buggy as he could, with the brim of his cap pulled low on his forehead. The horse plodded along Straight Road, head bowed against the harsh glare in the eastern sky.

True to its name, Straight Road ran due east across the Colorado prairie mile after monotonous mile. The land was flat, broken only by gullies and dry washes and low hills on the northern horizon. Spring had come. Aaron saw greening grasses and clumps of yellow blossoming rabbit brush.

Prairie dogs were active that morning. The rodent villages were marked by hundreds of mounds of dirt beside the prairie dog holes. As Aaron drew near a village beside the road, the prairie dogs would scamper to their holes, sit erect near the mounds of dirt, and sniff the air. Their forelegs stuck out like small hands above their round, prosperous bellies. Aaron waved his cap as he drove past one village and saw the prairie dogs dive into their holes, chirping in sudden panic. Overhead a hawk slowly circled, then flew away. Aaron supposed he had spoiled a morning's hunt.

At noon Aaron stopped beside the road. He watered the horse from his canteen and let the animal

graze while Aaron ate a meal of sardines and crackers. A family traveling in a covered wagon came down
the road. Aaron stopped them and asked if they
knew of the Coltrane road ranch on this road. The
man who drove the team said no, that he and his
family had come from Missouri and knew no one
out here. They planned to farm near Denver.

In the afternoon Aaron saw a few other travelers
on Straight Road. He asked each one about the Coltrane place, but none had heard of the name until
Aaron spoke to a freighter who was hauling a load
of dry goods.

"Coltrane," the big freighter said, turning his head
and spitting out a long stream of tobacco juice. "Sure,
I know where it is." He gestured over his shoulder.
"Sod house down the pike. I've never stopped there.
Can't afford them road ranches just for a hot meal
and a roof over my head." He spat again. "I don't
reckon Coltrane is doing much of a business anymore, though. Time was when there were five or six
road ranches along this stretch. Some offered more
than just a meal and a place to sleep, don't you
know?" He spat again and wiped the back of one
hand across his mouth. "Them days is gone, though.
Country's civilized now."

"How far is the Coltrane place from here?" Aaron
asked excitedly.

The freighter cast a suspicious look at Aaron's
rented horse. "Day's ride, maybe, for a fair-looking
gelding like that one." He nodded, as though con-
firming his own thoughts. "A day's ride from here, I
reckon."

"How many miles away from here?" Aaron asked.

"Dunno," the freighter said. "Never tried to figure
it. Hours are more important than miles in my work."

"What does the road ranch look like?" Aaron asked.

"Not much," the freighter said. "Just another sod house beside the road, long and low with a dirt roof, a couple windows in front. On the north side of the road. You'll come to it tomorrow afternoon, likely."

"Thanks," Aaron said, stepping back as the freighter spat again and reached for his whip. He popped the whip over the lead mules in the team of six. The big wagon lumbered away.

Aaron felt a great sense of excitement to learn that the road ranch still existed. He was anxious to get moving, but before he climbed back into the buggy, he pulled off his jacket. The day had grown warm. He tossed the jacket into the buggy. That was when he discovered he had failed to bring the revolver with him.

Chapter XIII

At sundown Aaron saw a grove of cottonwood trees on the horizon ahead. A herd of antelope grazed a couple of hundred yards away. They stopped grazing and watched Aaron for a time, then the lead buck flashed his white tail and bounded away toward the horizon. The rest of the herd, about thirty animals by Aaron's quick count, turned tail and followed.

Aaron wondered if the antelope had taken water in the grove, but then he saw a faint haze of smoke rise out of the treetops. A set of wheel ruts angled off Straight Road to the cottonwood grove. Aaron followed them. When he reached the edge of the grove, he called out.

"Hello, the camp!"

A lanky man wearing denim trousers, a dark flannel shirt, and a big Stetson came out of the trees. "Howdy."

"I'm looking for a place to water my horse," Aaron said. "And myself."

"Then climb out of that rig," he said, grinning. "There's good water here."

Aaron got out of the buggy and stretched his legs.

The man said, "I'm just passing through myself, but it appears this here water hole has been used by plenty of travelers." He held out his hand. "I'm Cal Tilburg."

Aaron introduced himself and shook hands. Tilburg was well over six feet tall, but Aaron doubted that he weighed more than 150 pounds. What Cal Tilburg lacked in girth, he made up for in talk. While Aaron unhooked the horse, Tilburg talked.

"I'm headed east, all the way back to Illinois," he said. "I stopped here to water Sunny and eat a bite. I'll light out in another hour or so. Ride all night, probably. Need a hand there?"

"No—" Aaron began.

"I run a little horse ranch up in the hills above Boulder. Know where that little town is?"

"Yes, I live in Den—"

"Yeah, I just got word my pa died. He owns, I should say owned, a farm out in Illinois where I growed up, and ma's still there. I'm the only kin she's got left. I aim to talk her into coming out here to live with me. Or at least live in Boulder, where she'll be around folks. I don't know if she'll leave that farm, though. Been on that ground all her life. It was first broke by her people, way back. Oh, she wanted me to stay there, but when I got some years on me, I had itchy feet. Wanted to try out things, know what I mean? I came out to Colorado. I worked up in the mines a spell, 'til I seen that moving dirt underground was no better than moving it on top. I always liked horses, though, so about ten years ago I took a string back into the hills. Been there ever since—selling, trading, and raising horses. I understand them, and they understand me, mostly. You bring that gelding back here to water. I'll show you a real running horse, ol' Sunny. I tell you I aim to make a fast ride back to Illinois. Say, that gelding's got a nice build. Yours?"

"No, I rented—"

"Yeah, he's not too bad for looks," Tilburg said. He quickly inspected the animal from teeth to tail. "Well, bring him back here."

Cal Tilburg walked along a path through the cottonwood trees. Aaron followed, leading the horse. In the center of the grove was a pond surrounded by a mud bank. The mud was speckled with the tracks of many animals—birds, coyotes, antelope, and horses. The gelding immediately walked through the mud to water's edge.

Aaron saw Cal Tilburg's camp on the far bank of the pond. A small fire burned within a circle of blackened stones. On the edge of the fire was a frying pan heaped with beans and bacon. A short distance away, tied to a tree, was a stallion.

Aaron was no judge of horses, and he had had practically no experience with saddle horses since the riding lessons he had taken at Hawkins Academy, but he could see that this stallion was a superior horse. The animal was big and well proportioned, long-legged and deep-chested. He nickered at the gelding and seemed to glare at Aaron and Cal Tilburg.

"That's a beautiful horse," Aaron said.

Tilburg grinned. "He's knows it, too. Got a hell of a temper-ment. Gets mean if I don't run him regular. He'll get plenty of running on this trip. Won't you, Sunny?" The stallion pulled tight against the rope that held him.

"Say," Tilburg said suddenly to Aaron, "why don't you sit down by my fire and take a bite of supper?"

"Thanks," Aaron said, "but I'm carrying plenty of—"

"Don't say no on account of being polite," Tilburg

said. "I've got more grub in the pan than I can get down. I always overdo when I get too hungry. Then I got to throw half of it out. Help me eat it up. I'd enjoy the company."

Aaron smiled. "All right, if you're sure you have enough to spare."

"I'm sure," Tilburg said. "Come on over here by my fire."

Aaron ate beans and bacon and listened to Cal Tilburg talk around great mouthfuls of food. He spoke at length of the many problems he encountered throughout the seasons of the year on his one-man horse ranch. Life was hard and lonely, Tilburg said, but he was generally happy. He speculated on the possibility of getting married someday.

"You a bachelor?" he asked.

Aaron nodded, although he had never thought of himself as a bachelor. The term sounded strange to his ear.

"A man ought to be married up, I reckon," Tilburg said thoughtfully. "Finding the right woman is the problem. I don't want no woman who's going to run my life or make me leave my ranch. No, sir." He shook his head slowly as he looked into the dying fire.

Tilburg did not remain silent for long. He went on to tell of the young man he had hired to look after his horses during his absence, then he launched into a long description of how Aaron could find the place. He insisted Aaron come for a visit. Tilburg expected to be home in two weeks.

Aaron agreed out of courtesy, but did not intend to do so.

After supper Cal Tilburg washed the frying pan and two metal plates in the pond, then broke camp.

Aaron watched him saddle the skittish stallion and mount up.

"Well, it's been real nice talking to you," Tilburg said, holding a tight rein on Sunny.

"Thanks for the—"

"I'll look for you to come a-visiting one of these days," Tilburg said. "Just look for the CT brand west of Boulder. So long."

Aaron stood back while the stallion pranced along the edge of the pond, throwing up great clods of mud and frightening the gelding. Tilburg good-naturedly cursed Sunny, then guided him along the trail through the cottonwoods, shouting good-by over his shoulder.

Aaron welcomed the evening's quiet after the drumming sounds of the running horse's hooves had died out. The long day in the buggy and Tilburg's relentless talk had left. Aaron exhausted. In the trees overhead birds sang evening songs until nightfall. Then coyotes began to call to one another. They were probably complaining that someone was monopolizing the water hole tonight, Aaron thought.

Aaron staked out the gelding at the edge of the mud bank, then brought a blanket from the buggy. He stretched out beside the glowing coals of the fire, wrapping the blanket around him. He looked up at the starry sky, closed his eyes, and suddenly blinked against sunlight.

Slept too long was Aaron's first thought that morning. The sun was still low in the eastern sky, casting shafts of light through the cottonwood trees. New leaves glistened green with the sunlight.

Aaron ate cold biscuits and jam for breakfast, then he hooked up the gelding to the buggy. He drove away from the grove along the wheel ruts that led to

Straight Road. Looking back, to the right of the grove, Aaron saw the herd of antelope. Led by the buck he had seen yesterday, the animals moved warily toward the water hole.

Aaron passed by several sod houses that morning. Most were off the road fifty to a hundred yards. All of them were obviously abandoned. Roofs had fallen in. Doors were missing or standing askew. And old farm roads off Straight Road were grown over with rabbit brush.

Hilly terrain lay ahead, like a giant washboard. Aaron drove over one gentle hill, another, and another in a seemingly endless succession. Some draws between the hills carried trickles of water. Lush grass grew in these places. Such growth, Aaron supposed, had tempted many homesteaders to try farming in the prairie. From the talk Aaron had heard in Denver, the early settlers had survived on antelope and jackrabbit stew for a few years, then quit.

Aaron ate his noon meal without stopping the buggy. He opened a can of sardines and ate them with crackers, then had a can of peaches. Among these prairie hills Aaron was aware of a strange, pervasive silence. He heard no breezes, no singing birds, no animal calls. The steady *clop-clop* of the horse's hooves and the creaking of the buggy sounded hauntingly loud.

An hour later Aaron topped a hill and drew back on the reins in surprise. In the draw ahead was a sod house. This one was occupied. A rectangle of prairie behind the house was freshly plowed. The plow stood at the edge of the field. In a nearby brush corral was a pair of draft horses.

The sod house was different in one respect from all the others Aaron had seen. This one was L-shaped.

Along the front wall were two small windows on either side of the door.

Behind the house was a slab shed, built of an odd assortment of boards stood on end. A stovepipe chimney stuck out of the shed's roof, leading Aaron to believe a forge was in there.

While Aaron watched, a man wearing a straw hat and overalls came out of the shed. He walked away from the sod house, along the edge of the plowed field. Aaron noticed that the man walked in a determined way, head thrust forward, and in one hand he carried a pair of long-handled tongs.

Aaron watched the man reach the end of the plowed field, climb up the hill across the draw, and disappear over the far side.

Aaron urged the horse ahead. At the bottom of the hill he turned off the road and let the gelding go to the water trough near the front of the sod house. Aaron got out of the buggy and stretched his legs. The windows in the sod house were dark rectangles. Aaron thought he glimpsed movement behind one, but could not be certain. He walked to the door and knocked.

The door opened slowly. Compared to the sun glare outside, the interior of the sod house seemed as dark as night. The man who cautiously peeked around the half-open door was puffy-faced and red-haired. Aaron recognized him.

They stared at one another for a long minute before a woman's voice came from inside the sod house.

"Close the door, Wally. You're letting flies in."

Wally did not move. His eyes were fixed on Aaron's. Aaron remembered seeing him that night he had looked into the drawing room. The stocky young man had stood against the edge of the fire-place, seemingly unaware of the scene of emotional violence between Harriet Armbrister and the white-haired man.

Presently a woman emerged from the darkness behind Wally, intent on closing the door, and in the next instant she looked at Aaron in surprise.

"Sadie Anne," Aaron said.

Her expression of surprise was replaced by one of recognition. "You . . . you . . ."

Aaron saw that her face was lined around her eyes and mouth. Her auburn hair was pulled back in a bun behind her head.

"Remember me?" he asked.

"What . . . what are you doing here?" she demanded suddenly. "How did you find me?"

Wally became agitated. He fidgeted and made gurgling sounds deep in his throat. He waved his hands clumsily, as though to push Aaron away.

"Wally," Sadie Anne said, stepping in front of him, "go inside. Go on, now." She guided Wally into the sod house, then she stepped out of the doorway and closed the door behind her. "You had no right to come here, Aaron. How did you find me?"

"That's a long story," Aaron said. "Want to hear it?"

She pursed her lips. "You must go away. Don't ever come back here."

Aaron could not keep anger out of his voice when he asked, "Why? Do I bring back too many memories?"

"Oh, Aaron," she said. She looked as though she had more to say, but then she turned and opened the door. Before she went into the sod house, she said, "Go away. Please, go away." She stepped into the sod house and closed the door. Aaron noticed that she was barefooted.

Aaron stood outside for several minutes. He felt confused and angry and somehow betrayed. For years he had imagined what would happen if he ever found Sadie Anne. In the theater of his mind he had acted out many scenes of his reunion with her. All of them were joyous and exciting.

Aaron turned away and returned to his buggy. He got in and took the reins. For a moment he looked back at the sod house. The black rectangles of the windows prevented him from seeing inside. The closed door seemed to be one of many through the years that had kept him from Sadie Anne.

Aaron made a decision. He turned the buggy, drove out to Straight Road, and headed west. He would give the appearance of leaving. But he was determined not to go away until he understood what had happened here, until he found the Sadie Anne he remembered.

Aaron drove over the hill. In the next draw, out of sight of the sod house, he turned north and drove through the brush and grass, parallel to the draw he had seen the straw-hatted man walk up. Fifty yards off Straight Road, Aaron stopped. He got out of the buggy and climbed the low hill. Near the top he dropped to his hands and knees and crawled. When he could see over the crest, he lay flat on his stomach.

From here he saw the back of the sod house. Another door opened out of the rear of the house, but there were no windows on this side. For nearly half an hour Aaron watched the house, the brush corral and shed, and he looked at the hill across the draw that he had seen the straw-hatted man walk over.

Movement at the rear of the sod house caught Aaron's eye. The back door swung open and Wally came outside. He closed the door and then trudged along the edge of the plowed field. Aaron saw that he retraced the steps of the first man as he climbed the hill and went over the other side.

Aaron debated whether to see what was over there, or go back to the sod house and confront Sadie Anne. Curiosity won out. Aaron got to his feet. He ran down the hill, crossed the draw, and sprinted up the hill beyond. Near the top he again crawled until he could see into the next draw.

The draw held another slab shed and two corrals. These were good, strong pole corrals. The largest contained eight or ten horses. In the second, smaller corral a horse had been thrown and tied down. The horse's head was covered with a burlap sack. A fire burned nearby.

Aaron watched the straw-hatted man and Wally as they knelt beside the fire. The straw-hatted man reached into the fire with the pair of tongs Aaron had seen him carrying. The man pulled a metal ring out of the fire. He carried it in to the corral. He touched the ring to the horse's flank. As smoke from burned hair and flesh rose up, Aaron realized that the man was using a running iron to alter the horse's brand.

When he finished, the man stepped back. He dropped the tongs and metal ring outside the corral, then took off his hat and wiped his brow. Before re-placing his hat, Aaron saw his long white hair and confirmed that this was the same man he had seen in the drawing room of the Armbrister mansion on the night of Harriet Armbrister's murder.

The man pulled the burlap sack off the horse's

flopping head. He cut the ropes that bound the animal's hooves. He quickly moved to the edge of the corral and ducked out between the poles.

The horse wiggled and leaped to his feet. He reared, pawing the air. With a shock, Aaron recognized the horse. It was Sunny, the big stallion owned by Cal Tilburg.

Chapter XIV

Horse thieves was the first thought that came into Aaron's mind. But as he observed the two men watch Sunny prance around the corral, a second thought ran a chill up his back: *Where was Cal Tilburg?*

Aaron tried to imagine reasonable circumstances that would explain what he saw. Perhaps the stallion had gone lame and Tilburg had stopped at the Coltrane road ranch to trade for another. But Aaron discarded the idea. He saw nothing wrong with Sunny. And there was only one reason to change the brand: to conceal theft.

Aaron's emotions stormed as he tried to think what he should do. Under other conditions, he would have left and gone straight to the U.S. marshal in Denver and reported what he had seen. But now Aaron was wracked with doubts.

A decision leaped to his mind. Aaron jumped to his feet and ran back down the hill. At the bottom he turned and sprinted alongside the field to the rear of the sod house. Barely hesitating, Aaron raised his boot and kicked in the back door. He heard a shriek inside. Aaron lunged in.

Sadie Anne stood in the kitchen, hands to her mouth, a look of terror on her face.

"It's all right," Aaron said, moving toward her.

For an instant he felt as though he were reliving an old dream. He had come to rescue Sadie Anne.

"I don't know what's going on here," Aaron said, "but I know that old man's a horse thief. I'm taking you away from here, and I'll come back with the United States marshal."

"Get out of here!" Sadie Anne screamed.

Aaron stopped. He stared at her.

Sadie Anne pleaded, "Go away, Aaron. Please."

Aaron felt too confused to speak. He glanced around the interior of the sod house. The walls were whitewashed. One end was devoted to the kitchen where there was a crude counter and a large iron stove. In the center of the room stood a plank table with benches on either side. The far end, at the bottom of the L, was curtained off. Through a gap in the curtain Aaron saw a hay-stuffed mattress covered by a colorful patchwork quilt.

Aaron looked at Sadie Anne. "Tell me what's going on here. Tell me what's happened to you." He added, "Then I'll leave."

Sadie Anne bowed her head but said nothing.

"I know some things about you," Aaron said. "I know your mother was named Sadie Anne Coltrane. Your father was Wallace Armbrister. He had two children by your mother. I would guess the other is the young man you called Wally. He's your brother."

Sadie Anne nodded slowly, still not looking up.

"And the white-haired man is your grandfather," Aaron said, "the father of Sadie Anne Coltrane."

"Yes," Sadie Anne whispered; then she looked up and said, "No."

Aaron shouted, "What is the truth?" He took a deep breath. "After you walked away from me that night, I tried to come after you, but the door was locked. Then I looked in a window and saw into the drawing room. Luke Coltrane and Wally were there—"

"Aaron, don't," Sadie Anne said. "I have nightmares."

Aaron moved a step closer to her. "I'll take you away from your nightmares."

Sadie Anne looked into Aaron's eyes; then her eyes widened as she turned her head slightly and looked past him.

Aaron turned around. Wally stepped through the back door. He carried an axe.

"Wally!" Sadie Anne shouted.

Aaron backed away as Wally advanced. Aaron ran into the plank table. His eyes were locked with Wally's. Aaron knew he would have to fight, but he felt paralyzed.

A crushing warmth at the back of Aaron's head made his knees go weak. A taste of blood shot to his mouth. He tumbled to the dirt floor as the image of Wally spun away from him. Sadie Anne's scream came from a great distance. Aaron was surrounded by darkness and a pressing silence that might have been death.

Aaron returned to life in darkness. He sat up, feeling a blast of pain jar his skull. He reached back and gingerly felt around the wound on the back of his head. Memory returned. He had been struck from behind, but he could not get the image of the axe out of his mind. Why wasn't he dead?

The darkness was absolute, or he had been struck blind. He sat upon a cold dirt floor. He felt around and found earthen walls on either side. For a moment he feared he had been buried alive.

Aaron got to his hands and knees. He raised up,

reaching overhead. His hand touched a rough beam, and another several inches away. The beams supported wood planks. Aaron crawled a short distance ahead, waving his hand into the thick darkness. He came to another dirt wall. Above he felt more planks, but no beams. He was beneath a trap door.

Aaron realized he was in a cellar of some kind. He pushed against the trap door, but it did not give. He got to his feet and put a shoulder against it. He pushed. His head pounded with pain. The door did not move.

Aaron rested, then crawled to the opposite end of the cellar. He found another trap door, but could not budge this one, either. Aaron sat down, head throbbing. He was frightened. *I'm blind*, he thought. *I'll never get out of here.*

Minutes or hours later—Aaron had no idea how long—the plank door above him slowly opened. He looked up into a starlit sky. *I can see!*

"Aaron," Sadie Anne whispered. "Aaron."

Aaron dimly saw her against the night sky as she stood over the open cellar door.

"Are you all right?" she whispered.

"I'm alive," Aaron said. He struggled to his feet, his head pounding.

Sadie Anne knelt and reached down. She found Aaron's arm. "Here, I'll help you."

Aaron pulled himself up and placed his arms outside on the ground. Sadie Anne pulled while he lifted himself. He got out far enough to swing a leg out. Aaron rolled out on the ground, sweating heavily and feeling dizzy.

"Drink this," Sadie Anne whispered.

Aaron sat up. Sadie Anne held a dipper. Aaron

took it and tipped it to his mouth. The cool water tasted good and refreshed him.

"You must leave," Sadie Anne whispered. "Quickly."

Aaron looked at her in the darkness. Her face was only a dim outline. The night concealed her expression. Aaron was reminded of the many nights he had been with her in the summerhouse. In those times he had no doubt that she loved him with the same fierce passion he felt for her. Now he wondered what the darkness had hidden from him.

Aaron got to his feet. "Why didn't he kill me?"

"He wanted to find out why you came here," Sadie Anne whispered. "What you knew." She stood up and walked away from him. In a moment she returned, leading a horse. "Wally saddled the stallion for you."

"Where's the buggy?" Aaron asked.

"I don't know what happened to it," she said. She whispered urgently, "Aaron, you must go away from here. Go away as fast as you can."

Aaron took the reins Sadie Anne held out for him. By starlight Aaron recognized Tilburg's stallion, Sunny.

"Why would Wally saddle a horse for me," Aaron asked, "after he tried to kill me?"

"Wally doesn't mean any harm," Sadie Anne said. "He thought you were trying to hurt me."

"Why do you stay here?" Aaron asked.

Sadie Anne whispered her brother's name. "Wally."

"What?" Aaron asked.

"I've saved him," she said. "I've saved him from the field of death." She pushed Aaron away and ran to the back door of the sod house. Aaron heard her go inside. Next he heard a deep, grumbling voice that came from within the house.

Aaron found the stirrup and swung up into the saddle. He guided the prancing horse around the house and past the water trough, just as the front door swung open. The banging door made Sunny shy away.

"Goddamn you!" Luke Coltrane bellowed.

In the darkness Aaron caught a glimpse of the white-haired man who lurched out of the doorway. The stallion reacted faster than Aaron could have. The animal took off at a run. Behind, Aaron heard a dull blast and realized Coltrane had fired a shotgun at him.

Aaron bent low over Sunny's neck and turned him west on Straight Road. The road was a pale ribbon on the starlit prairie hills. Another blast came from Coltrane's shotgun, but Aaron was out of range now.

The stallion ran hard, up the hill and down the far side, and up the next low hill. Aaron's head pounded every time Sunny's hooves struck the ground, but Aaron held on, clenching his teeth against the pain. Aaron knew that he must ride to Denver as fast as Sunny could go, and he knew that he must return to the Coltrane road ranch.

Aaron walked the stallion at intervals, but by daybreak both man and horse were close to exhaustion. Sometime in the night Aaron had passed the cottonwood grove. Aaron looked ahead, watching for signs of water. Presently he saw a small grove of trees off the road half a mile. He turned Sunny and rode toward it.

Aaron found that the cottonwoods did surround a small pool of murky water. Aaron dismounted, letting the stallion drink first. When he judged the horse had had enough, he pulled him away and let him graze on grass that grew nearby.

Aaron knelt at water's edge. He splashed water on his face. His head ached with dull pain now. When he reached back and felt the wound, his fingertips touched a large scab.

After sunup Aaron rode on. Sunny was eager to run, and Aaron let him go for a while, but he still pulled the horse down to a walk at intervals. He did not want to ride Sunny into the ground.

The outskirts of Denver came into view before noon. Aaron rode into the city, wondering if anyone would believe the ride he had made. In front of the Federal Building Aaron tied Sunny at a hitching post and went inside. He was so weak that he stumbled and nearly fell. He reached for the doorjamb and held on.

The clerk in the U.S. marshal's outer office looked up and then got to his feet. "My God, what happened to you?"

Aaron gained his footing and walked into the office. "I want to see Burns."

The clerk nodded. He turned and went into the marshal's office. He soon returned.

"He'll see you now."

Aaron walked past the clerk and entered Burns's office. The U.S. marshal stared at Aaron. He gestured to a chair in front of his desk. "Sit down, Mills."

Aaron collapsed into the chair.

"You'd better see a doctor," Burns said.

"I will," Aaron said, "but I've got something to tell you."

"Let's hear it," Burns said.

Aaron gave the marshal a brief account of his research into the Armbrister story, and the information he had uncovered that led to the discovery of the Coltrane road ranch. He told of meeting Cal Tilburg on the way, and of the corrals that were out of sight of the road ranch. Aaron described Luke Coltrane, Wally, and Sadie Anne, and told how he had been clubbed from behind.

"That's a wild tale, Mills," Marshal Burns said. He got up and came around his desk. He examined Aaron's head wound. "You sure got your skull busted, all right." Burns picked up his hat. "Let's go take a look at that horse."

Aaron stood too quickly and was nearly knocked over by a wave of dizziness. Burns took his arm.

"I'm all right," Aaron said, trying to smile.

"The hell," Burns said. "You need a doctor."

"Not yet," Aaron said, pulling away from him. "Come on outside."

Sunny was lathered and his head drooped. Burns walked around the horse and examined the altered brand.

"Not a bad job," Burns said. "By the time it heals and some of the hair grows back, you'd never know that was a CT brand."

Aaron said, "I need to get that horse to a livery so he can be fed and rubbed down."

Burns untied the horse's reins. "I'll take him, Mills. We'll need him for evidence. Now, you go hunt up a doctor, hear?"

Aaron nodded. Before leaving, he gave instructions on how to find the road ranch, a description of the place, and the location of the corrals where he had seen the horses.

Aaron walked to the corner and caught a trolley

that took him close to the *Denver City Journal*. From the way the other passengers stared, Aaron realized he must look as though he had just climbed out of the grave. Perhaps he had. Aaron had no doubt that Luke Coltrane intended to murder him.

Aaron climbed the stairs to the *Journal* office, clenching his teeth against the jarring pain in his head. A few reporters were in the main office, including Homer Witt. The editor-in-chief was conferring with Henry Daniels. Both men looked up at Aaron in shock. A hush fell over the office.

Witt recovered first. He rushed to Aaron. "What happened to you?"

"I feel better than I look," Aaron said.

Witt took his arm. "Daniels, help me with him."

Daniels crossed the office and grasped Aaron's other arm. The two men led Aaron into Witt's office and placed him in a chair. Witt opened a lower drawer of his desk and brought out a bottle of brandy. He pulled the cork and poured some into a coffee-stained cup. He handed the cup to Aaron. "Drink it," Witt said.

Aaron tipped the cup to his mouth. The liquor burned his throat as it went down. He coughed. A spasm of pain shot through his head, bringing tears to his eyes.

Witt moved behind Aaron. "That's quite a wound. Doc Ames better look at it." He came around in front of Aaron. "What the hell happened?"

Aaron told Witt and Daniels and all the reporters who had come into the office what happened when he reached the Coltrane road ranch. When he finished, Daniels spoke up.

"I'll put Sam Catton on this one. He should be able to catch up with the posse." Daniels turned and started out of the office, elbowing his way through the reporters.

"Not so fast, Daniels," Witt said. He looked at Aaron. "This is your story. You broke it open. You can cover it if you want it."

"I want it," Aaron said, "but I won't be able to move fast enough to be on the scene when the posse gets out there. Somebody else had better go."

"All right," Witt said. He looked at Daniels and nodded. "Go find Sam."

"That's where I was headed," Daniels said irritably. He stomped out of the office.

Witt took Aaron by the arm and helped him out of the chair. "I'll take you home, Aaron."

The brandy began to take effect. Aaron felt very agreeable and sleepy-eyed tired. He leaned against Homer Witt as they left the office, descended the back stairs, and got into his buggy. Witt drove to the boarding house while Aaron fought to stay awake.

Homer Witt helped Aaron to his room in the boarding house, then left, promising to return with the doctor. Aaron pulled off his clothes and washed. He crawled into bed. He thought he had just closed his eyes for a moment when he was awakened by Homer Witt.

"This is Dr. Ames," Witt said, pointing to a short, round-faced man who was opening his black bag. Ames came to the other side of the bed and examined the wound.

"Bad?" Witt asked.

"I'll have to trim away some hair before I can tell," Ames said. "Hold still, young man. What were you slugged with?"

"I don't know," Aaron said. "I didn't see it coming."

Dr. Ames snipped hair around the wound. He washed it with alcohol and bandaged it.

"I didn't find any bone chips," Ames said to Aaron. "Still, your skull might be cracked. With a head wound, you have to be careful. Your brain took a powerful blow. Further activity might cause damage. I want you to stay in bed for at least two weeks. Four weeks would be better."

Aaron groaned at the thought of that.

"He'll do it," Homer Witt said, "if I have to tie him down."

Witt accompanied Dr. Ames to the door. They briefly discussed an upcoming poker game, then Ames said he would return in two or three days to change the bandage. After he was gone, Witt came to Aaron's bedside.

"Do what the doc tells you," Witt said. "Don't move around any more than is absolutely necessary."

Aaron did not want to agree, nor did he want to lie to Homer Witt, so he said nothing.

"Sleep is what you need," Witt said. He put on his hat. "I'll come back tomorrow afternoon and look in on you."

"Thanks," Aaron said.

Witt said good-by and went to the door. He had no sooner closed the door when he opened it again and leaned into the room. "More company, Aaron."

Aaron sat up. Mae Catton stood in the doorway.

Chapter XV

"Come in, Mae," Aaron said.

Witt waved good-by to Aaron and closed the door after Mae entered the room. She came to Aaron's bedside and looked at him as though wondering whether he would live.

"I heard you were hurt when I delivered Daddy's copy to the *Journal*," she said. She leaned over Aaron and looked at the bandage on the back of his head. "How do you feel?"

"My head aches a little," Aaron said.

"Tell me what happened out there," Mae said.

Aaron smiled. "Mae, you don't have to look so solemn. I'm all right."

"You should not have gone out there alone," she said, shaking her head. "I shouldn't have let you."

"How would you have stopped me," Aaron asked lightly, "with that little revolver?"

"Why didn't you use it?" she asked.

"I didn't have the thing," Aaron said. "I went off and forgot it."

Mae's face twisted as though she might cry.

"Mae, I was hit from behind," Aaron said. "The revolver wouldn't have done me any good." As Aaron spoke, he realized that if he had taken the gun, he would have shot Wally.

Mae sat on the edge of the bed. "Well, tell me exactly what happened. Did you find Sadie Anne?"

Aaron told her what he had seen at the Coltrane road ranch, leaving out a few details such as Sadie Anne's obscure mention of a "field of death."

"What was she like?" Mae asked of Sadie Anne.

Aaron thought a moment. "She wasn't the Sadie Anne that I remembered." He added, "I guess she's had a hard life."

"Everyone changes in time," Mae said.

"Sadie Anne was more than just changed," Aaron said. He tried to find words to elaborate, but could not.

"You might have had her built up in your mind in a certain way," Mae said.

The remark stung Aaron. He looked away, then said, "I'm going back there tomorrow."

"Aaron, you can't!" Mae exclaimed. "You're hurt. You need to stay in bed."

"Everybody's telling me that today," Aaron said.

"You should listen," Mae scolded.

"I'm all right," Aaron said. "If something was seriously wrong with me, the ride back to Denver would have finished me."

"You're mule stubborn," Mae said. She looked down at him. "Are you worried about Sadie Anne? Will she be arrested?"

"I don't know," Aaron said. "I don't know what will happen. Luke Coltrane is a wild man."

Mae announced, "I'm going with you."

Aaron sat up, wincing against the pain that shot through his head. "No, you aren't."

Mae stood. "There's no use in arguing. I'm going. In fact, I am taking you with me. Tonight I'll pack some food. In the morning I'll rent a buggy and come here and get you."

"Mae—"

She smiled as she repeated a question Aaron had posed: "How will you stop me—with that little revolver?"

Early in the morning Aaron was awakened from a deep sleep by loud, repeated knocks on his door. He got out of bed and stumbled to the door. He found Mae in the hall, dressed for traveling.

"Are you still determined to go?" she asked.

Aaron mumbled that he was.

"I'll be waiting outside," Mae said.

Head throbbing, Aaron went back into his room. He shaved and dressed. He gathered up a change of clothes, picked up his boots, and walked outside in his stocking feet. He found Mae sitting on the padded leather seat of a Concord buggy, with the top up.

"How's your head?" Mae asked as she watched Aaron climb into the buggy.

"Still there," Aaron said.

"I rented the best buggy I could find," Mae said, "so you'll be as comfortable as possible."

Aaron nodded and thanked her, but he thought she should have been more concerned about the horse. A small chestnut mare pulled the buggy. *This trip will be a slow one,* Aaron thought.

Mae urged the mare ahead and drove down the street. The sun had just come up. Aaron gave Mae directions until she got on the street that led to Straight Road. Then he leaned against Mae and rested his head on her shoulder. The motion of the buggy was somehow comforting. So was the presence of Mae.

Aaron jerked awake when the buggy came to a halt. He looked out on the prairie, then he looked at Mae. She smiled.

"Time to eat," she said. "How are you feeling?"

"I don't know yet," Aaron said. He got out of the buggy. A dull pain was in the back of his head, like a bad memory. "Better," he said. "I'm feeling better now."

"Good," Mae said. She reached behind the buggy seat. From under a pile of blankets she brought out a wicker basket.

"I hope you like cold chicken and potato salad," she said as she climbed out of the buggy.

Aaron realized he was ravenously hungry. He and Mae walked a short distance away from the Concord buggy and sat on the ground. Aaron wolfed down three pieces of chicken, two biscuits with honey, and nearly half of the potato salad.

Half an hour later they drove on. Mae still insisted on taking the reins. Aaron rode beside her for a while, but presently he began feeling sleepy again. He twisted around in the seat and put his head in her lap.

Before dropping off to sleep, he said, "Mae, you're quite a woman."

"Sure, I am," she said. "I give you food and a pillow."

Aaron remembered wishing she would take his words more seriously, and for a moment he thought of trying to explain how his perception of her had changed, how she had transformed from girl to woman almost before his eyes, but then sleep overcame him. When he again opened his eyes in the gently rocking buggy, he sat up and saw that the sun was low in the western sky.

"I've slept all day," Aaron said in surprise. He stretched and then massaged his neck several times before he realized that his head no longer ached.

"My headache's gone!" he exclaimed.

Mae said dully, "That's good."

Aaron looked at her, at once knowing she must be exhausted from driving the buggy all day. He took the reins from her.

"I'll take over," he said. "It's your turn to lean against me. Get some sleep."

Without a protest she did so. Soon she was asleep in Aaron's lap.

Aaron stopped before nightfall to rest and water the mare, but he was not ready to make camp. After an hour he drove on, eating a piece of cold chicken and watching night come to the prairie.

Aaron judged the time to be about midnight when he pulled off the road a short distance and stopped the buggy. Mae woke up.

"Where are we?" she asked.

"I'm not sure," Aaron said, peering into the darkness, "but we should be near the hill country where the Coltrane place is. We'll get some sleep and then go on in the morning."

"I brought blankets," Mae said. She turned and rummaged around behind the buggy seat. She brought out two heavy wool blankets. While Aaron unhooked the mare and hobbled her, Mae found a flat place on the ground and spread the blankets.

They lay side by side, wrapped in the blankets, and looking up at the night sky. Aaron turned on his side and spoke to Mae.

"The first time I saw you, I thought you were just a girl—a tall child who was dependent on her father. I was wrong. I think Sam is dependent on you."

Mae said nothing for a while. "I don't think Daddy was ready for me to grow up for a long time. He wanted me to be that same girl in pigtails who was eager to run errands for him after school every day, fix supper when he felt like coming home, and then have breakfast ready in the morning. We were partners, and he did not want that to change."

"But you told me he bought you new clothes," Aaron said, "and said it was time for you to look like a lady."

"I lied," Mae said. "I said those things to Daddy. I was getting too big, too womanly to be running around like a freckle-faced girl."

"Tell me about your mother," Aaron said.

"I can't," Mae replied. "I never knew her. She died in childbirth." She added, "Changes. Everybody changes, Aaron, all the time."

The sky was black and deep and filled with stars. Aaron listened to Mae's soft breathing and thought of changes. He wondered how much he had changed. *Not much*, was his first thought. He felt now about the same as he always had. He had a strong sense of determination. Perhaps that was why he had been successful. Aaron recalled that Homer Witt had said a man's father was often responsible for the son's later successes. Perhaps so. Jacob Mills was a hard worker.

But Aaron suspected he might have inherited traits of stubbornness and determination from his mother. And the influence of Charley Simms had been strong, and that influence had come at a crucial time. Charley Simms had taught Aaron how to work and how to get a job done.

In one sense, Aaron felt a great sense of personal awareness. He knew why he was in this eastern

Colorado prairie now, and he had an inkling of a dark secret that might be uncovered tomorrow, but a larger question lurked in Aaron's mind. Or perhaps under this night sky he became aware of many questions that were woven into a larger one, questions of his own heritage, his boyhood love of Sadie Anne, the mystery of her, and then his own success in school and later on the staff of the *Denver City Journal*. The question at the end that loomed large as Aaron stared into the heavens was simply *Who am I?*

Before sunup Aaron and Mae broke camp. They ate a cold breakfast. The eastern sky was reddening when they climbed into the buggy and drove out to Straight Road. In less than two hours they reached the hill country. At midmorning they topped the hill that overlooked the Coltrane road ranch.

Aaron expected to find the posse here, but he saw no one around the sod house and only one horse was in the brush corral. As he drove down the hill and into the yard, Marshal Burns came out of the sod house, limping.

"I didn't expect to see you here, Mills," the marshal said, glancing at Mae. "You ever go to a doctor?"

Aaron nodded. "You look like you need a doctor."

"Got thrown," Burns said, trying to smile. "I'm not the horseman I used to be."

Aaron climbed out of the buggy and helped Mae down. "Where's your posse?" Aaron asked.

"Out in the hills," Burns said, "chasing the Coltranes. We missed them by a few hours, near as I can tell. Found hot ashes in the stove. Looks like they left most of their possessions behind in the house. We found a couple horses in the corral over the hill back there."

"There were eight or ten when I was here," Aaron said.

Burns nodded. "We saw plenty of tracks leading away. Coltrane probably took the best with him."

Mae asked, "Where's Sam Catton?"

Burns squinted at her. "He rode with one of the groups I sent. One bunch tried to trail the stolen horses. I sent the others due north, hoping they could overtake the Coltranes. You're Sam's daughter, aren't you?"

"Yes," Mae said.

"I thought I recognized you," Burns said. "Sam will be back by noon. I told all the men to come back by noon today if they hadn't found any sign." Burns looked back at the sod house. "Funny thing in there. A trap door opens to some kind of cellar or tunnel. It leads underground twelve or fifteen feet, then there's another door outside that looks like it might have been covered over with dirt."

"That's where I was when I came to," Aaron said. "I've got a feeling that's where Cal Tilburg is, too."

"What do you mean?" Burns asked.

"Come on and I'll show you," Aaron said. "Is there a shovel around here?"

Marshal Burns and Mae followed Aaron around the sod house to the shed in back. Inside was a bellows and forge. Animal traps hung on the walls, along with an assortment of tools and horseshoes. In one corner Aaron found a spade.

Aaron carried the spade to the trap door behind the house. He pulled the big door open and dropped the shovel in, then climbed into the hole himself.

Aaron looked up at Mae. "Go back to the buggy."

"What?" Mae asked in surprise.

"Go on back to the buggy," Aaron said.

Mae pursed her lips. "I will not."

Aaron glared at her, then began digging in the cellar floor. He dug down nearly two feet in several places. He found nothing but more dirt. His head began to throb. At last he tossed the shovel out, and climbed out of the hole.

"What did you expect to find," Burns asked, "a corpse?"

Aaron nodded. He had been certain he was right, and now he felt confused. Nothing was buried in that cellar; the dirt was packed hard. He looked at the sod house, then turned and looked out across the plowed field . . . suddenly he knew.

"That field is plowed and harrowed," Aaron said, "but nothing is growing there."

"Maybe he planted late," Marshal Burns said. "Or maybe he didn't plant at all this year."

Aaron walked to the edge of the field and began digging again. Digging was much easier in this loose soil. He made a narrow trench, nearly two feet deep. He dug in a straight line for twenty or twenty-five feet, then came back half that distance and dug at a right angle.

Marshal Burns and Mae watched in silence as Aaron dug the second trench. Still, he found nothing. Aaron stopped and came back to the first trench. He began digging in the opposite direction. This time he worked only a few minutes when he uncovered a shoe.

Aaron carefully shoveled dirt away from the shoe and black broadcloth above it. More digging revealed another shoe and a man's leg.

"My God!" Burns said.

Mae's hands flew to her mouth as Aaron uncovered the lower torso of a man. In a few minutes the whole body was exposed, face down in the field.

"Tilburg?" Burns asked.

Aaron shook his head. "No."

Burns took the shovel from Aaron and turned the body over. The flesh was decomposed. The top of the skull was split open. Mae fled.

Burns looked out across the field. "Tilburg must be buried out there." He looked up at Aaron. "My God, Mills, how many more are buried out there?"

Aaron said, "A field of death."

The two of them, trading off with the spade, began systematically digging up the field. Within an hour they had uncovered the body of Cal Tilburg. His skull was split open, too.

Before noon three more bodies were unearthed. All of them were men and all had been murdered in the same way. Aaron and Marshal Burns dragged each body to the edge of the field, and left them there side by side. At first Aaron had felt sick to his stomach, but that passed and now he felt numbed. They had dug up less than a fourth of the plowed field.

Shortly past noon the first group of men in the posse returned. They were soon followed by the remaining men. All of them expressed the same shock and disbelief that had been Aaron's and Marshal Burns's first reactions.

The men in the posse began digging. A second shovel was found, and two men carried short-handled shovels with their gear. All of the men traded off with the four shovels.

Mae had been upset, but now she was distressed. Sam Catton had not come in with the posse. She asked several men where he was. Finally one told her that Catton had become convinced they were on a wild goose chase and had ridden back to Denver.

"But we didn't see him on Straight Road," Mae said.

"We was up north," the man said. "Sam took off across the prairie, headed west."

All of the men were tired from many hours in the saddle and a dry camp last night. Aaron spoke to several of them and learned they had lost the tracks of the horses in rocky country. Their frustration now turned to anger with the grisly task at hand.

"The Coltranes should be lynched," one man with a flowing mustache said. "Slow."

Others agreed. The Coltranes were mad dogs who should be hunted down and killed.

More corpses were found. All of them were badly decomposed. Some were only skeletons covered with rotting cloth. By evening the total count of bodies was at nineteen. The entire field had been excavated.

A bonfire was built that night in front of the sod house. The flames were fed by the furnishings inside the house. The plank table and benches were burned, along with all the quilts and bedding. One of the men found a can of whitewash in the slab shed. He painted KILLER COLTRANES in huge letters on the front of the sod house. Bottles of whiskey appeared and were circulated as the men stood around the great blaze. Aaron took down their names and spoke to each man briefly, but he did not record the chief topic of conversation: the slowest way to kill the Coltranes.

Privately, Burns said to Aaron and Mae, "My duty is to bring in the Coltranes alive. After what these men have seen today, I'd have trouble doing my duty if we did catch up with the Coltranes."

With the help of a torch and two men from the posse, Aaron found his rented buggy in the next draw. The gelding was gone, apparently stolen by Luke Coltrane. Aaron managed to hitch the little buggy to the back of the Concord. The arrangement meant slow going for the mare, but Aaron saw no alternative. Both he and Mae were eager to leave.

Half a moon came up. By the light of it, Aaron and Mae drove away from the Coltrane road ranch and the bonfire that burned in front of it. Looking back once, Aaron saw the ghostly men who stood around the flames and the words printed in large white letters on the front of the sod house: KILLER COLTRANES. The image stuck in Aaron's mind all night as he drove.

By moonlight Aaron found the cottonwood grove where he met Cal Tilburg. Aaron turned off the road and drove to it. As the moonlit trees drew near, Aaron felt a chill run up his spine. What if the Coltranes had hidden here?

Aaron tried to push the fear away as he stopped the buggy. Mae woke up.

"Wait here," Aaron said. He got out of the buggy. He moved slowly into the grove, listening for sounds. He heard nothing. Near the pond that now reflected moonlight, Aaron felt uneven ground beneath his feet. The soft earth had been worked up by many animals—horses, probably.

At first Aaron felt relieved. The posse had been here. But then again Aaron wondered if Luke Coltrane had watered his stolen horses in the grove. Aaron walked around the pond, at last convinced no one was here.

Aaron returned to the buggy and unhooked the mare. He led her to water. Mae followed with the wicker basket and blankets. They ate in silence around the charred remains of the campfire Cal Tilburg had made.

Chapter XVI

Aaron got up at the first light of day. His head ached dully. He had slept little. Aaron moved quietly as he filled the canteens, watered the mare, and hooked her up to the Concord buggy. Then he awakened Mae. She leaned sleepily against him as he led her to the waiting buggy.

Aaron drove all the way to Denver, stopping to rest the mare frequently. They reached the city early in the evening. Mae had been quiet for most of the journey, but as they neared Denver, Aaron noticed that she became more alert, apparently anxious to see her father.

Aaron dropped off the buggy at the City Livery and explained to the liveryman that the gelding had been stolen. The liveryman accepted a deposit from Aaron and two local references: Homer Witt and Marshal Burns. Then Aaron returned the Concord to the livery where Mae had rented it.

They caught a trolley and rode to Union Station. In the gathering darkness Aaron walked Mae home. A lamp burned in a window of the Catton home.

"Good night, Mae," Aaron said.

She looked up at him in the half light of late evening. Aaron brought his mouth down to hers, kissed her lightly, then turned and walked away.

"Good night, Aaron," Mae said after him.

Aaron returned to Union Station and rode a trolley that ran near the *Denver City Journal* building. Aaron walked to the back door and let himself in with his key. He felt tired yet strangely alert. He lit a lamp and took it to his desk. He wanted to get the Coltrane story written, as though the act of writing an account of what he had seen in the last few days would somehow purge his system of the pain and anguish he felt Aaron headlined the story "Field of Death," and began writing.

Aaron was awakened by an angry Homer Witt. Witt came into Aaron's office early in the morning.

"Where the hell have you been?"

Aaron sat up, blinking against the light of day. The lamp on his desk burned low on the wick.

Witt said, "I went to your room yesterday. You were gone."

Aaron handed him the story he had written last night. Witt glared at Aaron as if Aaron's silence represented defiance; then he turned his attention to the story.

Witt read through the pages rapidly. When he finished, he looked at Aaron in shock and disbelief.

"Nineteen men . . . murdered," Witt said slowly. "How did Coltrane get away with it?"

"All the victims were like Cal Tilburg, I imagine," Aaron said. "Lone travelers. Coltrane murdered them for their possessions. Friends or relatives might miss them, but where would they look?"

"You think they were murdered in the sod house," Witt said, "and then dragged outside through that cellar?"

Aaron nodded. "Coltrane probably carried his victims out to the field after dark and buried them.

The next day he could cover any trace of the grave with a harrow."

"That girl you were looking for," Witt said. "What did she have to do with it?"

"I don't know," Aaron said. He added, "Nothing, I hope."

"But she must have had knowledge of the killings," Witt said. Without waiting for a reply, Witt motioned to the bandage on Aaron's head. "How do you feel?"

"Tired," Aaron said. "I could sleep a week."

"You go home and do that, then," Witt said. "I'm sorry I snapped at you. I had no idea of what you've been through."

Aaron said, "I knew that if I told you what I planned, you'd have stopped me—or tried to."

"Damned right, I would have," Witt said. "You'll kill yourself at this rate." He paused, then looked at the story Aaron had written. "I'll give you credit for one thing. You've busted open a big story. You may not know it yet, but you've made a name for yourself."

Aaron went home when most people were coming to work. He crawled into bed and slept all day. Late in the afternoon Dr. Ames came to change the bandage. The old one was dirty and caked with blood.

"I see you're not a man to follow doctor's orders," Ames said.

"I had some important business to take care of," Aaron said.

"You have your health to take care of, young man," Dr. Ames said. "At your age you take good health for granted, like a permanent gift. It isn't, believe me. Lose your good health and you'll have no one to blame but yourself."

Ames bathed the wound and put on a fresh bandage. When he was done, Aaron asked what the charge was.

"Plenty," Ames said, "but I've been requested to send the bill elsewhere."

"Where?" Aaron asked in surprise.

"To Homer Witt," Ames said. "In case you don't know it, Witt is not only a hell of a poker player, he's also a man who feels an obligation to his employees." Ames turned, picked up his bag, and marched to the door. Before going out, he said, "Good evening, young man. Live a long life."

"Thank you, Doctor," Aaron said. After Ames had gone, Aaron tried to sleep again. He craved peace and quiet. He did not get it.

An hour later Aaron answered a loud, steady pounding on his door. In the hall he found a red-faced, whiskey-smelling Sam Catton.

"Mills, you pulled that Coltrane story right out from under me."

"Sam, I didn't know—"

"Don't lie to me," Catton shouted, staggering as he spoke. "I got the whole tale out of Mae. You've been on this story for a long time. You knew a hell of a lot more than you ever told me. You sent me out there on the prairie so I'd make a fool out of myself."

"No, you did that yourself, Sam," Aaron said, his own voice rising in anger. "If you'd come back to the Coltrane place—"

"If I'd had more information, I would have!" Catton shouted. His breath grew ragged and he leaned against the wall. He swallowed hard. "And what's the idea of dragging my daughter out there to see that?"

"I didn't want her to go," Aaron said. "If you'd ask her, she'd tell you."

"Oh, she told me, all right," Catton said, "but I can't believe a big strong fellow like you couldn't have stopped her."

"I could have stopped her from going with me," Aaron said, "but I couldn't have stopped her from following me. She was determined to go. I think she was worried about you."

"Oh, hell," Catton said. "She went on your account. And you were alone with my girl for two nights. . . ."

"What are you trying to say, Sam?" Aaron asked. He stared Catton down.

"Well, you've landed a front page story again, Mills," Catton said. "I suppose you know where the Coltranes went, too."

"No, I don't," Aaron said, realizing too late that the question was a sarcastic one.

Sam Catton grinned crookedly at Aaron. In a low voice he said, "Stay the hell away from my daughter, Mills. Stay away from her, or I'll kill you."

Catton straightened up and walked down the hall, weaving slightly. Aaron saw him square his shoulders and hold his arms straight against his sides in a way that was almost comical.

In the following days Homer Witt's prediction came true. Aaron had made a name for himself. His story on the front page of the *Denver City Journal* became the basis for published accounts of the Coltrane murders throughout the country.

And the story quickly became sensationalized. The *Police Gazette* added line drawings depicting a fanciful murder scene in a sod house on the Colorado prairie, and speculated that dozens of other bodies were buried in the surrounding hills.

The words "Killer Coltranes" became a common phrase. Sightings of a white-haired man accompanied by an idiot boy and a beautiful young woman became commonplace, too. Rumors that the Coltranes were "murderous cannibals" who roamed the West in search of lone travelers were published as facts in many newspapers. Within two weeks the task of separating fact from fiction became nearly impossible.

Of the nineteen bodies, only three were ever identified positively. Relatives identified two of the recent murder victims in a Denver morgue. One skeleton was later discovered to be that of a woman, leading Aaron to believe it was the remains of Sadie Anne Coltrane.

For the benefit of Marshal Burns, Aaron identified the body of Cal Tilburg. Aaron wrote a letter to the Boulder newspaper asking information from anyone who knew where Cal Tilburg's mother lived in Illinois.

Aaron's own mother wrote him a flurry of letters when the Coltrane story broke in California. She alternately chided Aaron for risking his life and praised him for being so successful in his work. Her son was famous, she wrote. Predictably, she closed many of her letters by recommending that Aaron marry and produce children so that (1) he would continue the Mills line, and (2) he would be as happy as Jennifer was.

Due to great pressure from the citizenry, the state of Colorado posted a $10,000 reward for the capture of the Coltranes. With that, "sightings" of the trio mushroomed. And on at least two occasions, white-haired old men were arrested and jailed.

Perhaps by writing the story, Aaron had purged himself. He felt somehow removed from all the talk of the Coltranes. And he was certainly bored with all the requests he received to recount his experiences. He no longer felt a compulsion to find Sadie Anne. Indeed, he now had doubts that she was still alive.

One afternoon Mae came into his office. "Daddy didn't mean what he said to you last week," she said. "He was drinking."

Aaron nodded that he understood.

"He's quit," Mae said. She added, "Again."

"I'm glad to hear that," Aaron said.

Mae's voice broke when she said, "Aaron, I'm sorry that he threatened you."

"I didn't take him seriously," Aaron said. "I have his gun, remember?"

Mae did not smile at the remark. "Daddy wants to apologize to you, Aaron. Will you let him?"

"Of course," Aaron said.

"Then he'll be here tomorrow afternoon," Mae said. She moved to the door, then turned back. "Aaron, I want you to know that I told Daddy you knew some things about the Coltranes, but I did not reveal any of the details you told me in confidence. I could not stand it if you thought I had betrayed your confidence."

"I don't," Aaron said, but in truth he had been annoyed by the thought that she had told Sam "the whole tale." He smiled at Mae.

Mae did not return the smile. "Daddy will be here tomorrow afternoon, then," she repeated.

Aaron could not help but think, *I'll believe that when I see him.* The specter of Sam Catton coming here to apologize did not come easily to mind. But twenty-four hours later Aaron was glad he had kept his doubts to himself. Sam Catton came into Aaron's office, hat in hand.

"I made a fool out of myself, Mills," he said. "I'm sorry. I'm damned sorry."

"I hold no hard feelings, Sam," Aaron said.

Catton looked at Aaron a moment. "You accept my apology?"

"Yes," Aaron said. "Now, let's forget the past."

Catton nodded slowly. "I should be thrashed for what I said to you. Hell, I'd never kill anyone." He added, "Not even you." He turned and walked out of the office, leaving the door open behind him.

Aaron realized Sam Catton did hold hard feelings. Aaron wondered if he was still angry over the Coltrane story, or the fact that Aaron had been with his daughter for three days.

Aaron caught Mae later in the afternoon when she delivered her father's copy to the city editor's basket. She knew her father had apologized and was happy. Aaron suspected Sam Catton had done his daughter's bidding, but did not ask. He had another request in mind.

"You fed me well out there on the prairie," Aaron said. "Now, let me return the favor."

"How?" Mae asked, smiling.

"By taking you to the Brown Palace Hotel dining room," Aaron said, "and treating you to the best meal on the menu."

Mae took his hand. "All right. I'll put on my best new dress."

The dinner date was a great success as Aaron came to understand that a bond existed between him and Mae because of the experiences they shared.

Conversation came easily, and Aaron found himself talking to her about the future. After taking Mae home and kissing her good night, Aaron returned to his boarding house, feeling happier than he had in a long time.

The next morning Homer Witt came into Aaron's office. "There's been a murder at the Armbrister mansion," he said.

Chapter XVII

"Murder," Aaron said in surprise.

"A body was discovered inside the mansion this morning," Witt said.

"I thought the police were guarding the mansion," Aaron said.

"That didn't last long," Homer Witt said. "Marshal Greene protested to the mayor that he was short-handed and he couldn't afford to keep policemen in the mansion around the clock without sacrificing law enforcement on the streets. So now the Armbrister property is patrolled—which means a policeman goes up there once in a while to see how much vandalism has been done." Witt paused. "I want you to cover this story, Aaron."

Aaron stood and put on his light coat. "I'll go right away." He did not ask the question that came to his mind: Why hadn't this story been given to Sam Catton?

The Armbrister property was cordoned off by policemen. Aaron joined half a dozen other reporters outside the front gate. He overheard one speculate that the ghost of Wallace Armbrister had committed murder now. The remark brought laughter from the others.

Marshal Greene came out of the mansion and stood

on the portico. He appeared to be waiting for some-one. A journalist called out, "Hey, Floyd, let us in."

Greene waved at the man to be patient. Behind the journalists a buggy rolled in to the drive. Aaron saw U.S. Marshal Burns get out. He came toward the gate, still limping on the leg he had injured when he had been thrown from the horse on the way to the Coltrane road ranch.

"What's going on, Marshal?" one of the journalists asked. "This is a federal case?"

Burns looked at the group of men. He saw Aaron. "Mills, come with me."

"Hey," another journalist protested, "if he goes in, we all go."

Burns looked at the man. "In ten minutes you can all come in."

Aaron walked through the gate and past the policemen with Burns. Behind him he heard one of the journalists say, "Some newshounds get better treatment than others."

At the portico Marshal Burns and Aaron were greeted by Greene. They entered the mansion and walked down the hall. They passed the damaged wall and entered the drawing room.

The corpse lay before the fireplace hearth, face down, amid debris of wood and canvas. Aaron saw the deep wound in the red-haired skull and recalled vividly the first time he had ever seen a murder victim: Mrs. Harriet Armbrister. She had been killed in the same manner.

"I thought you ought to see this," Greene said to Marshal Burns, "since you investigated the Coltrane killings."

Burns nodded. "Same type of wound." He looked at Aaron. "Looks like a Coltrane killing, doesn't it?"

"Yes," Aaron said.

Burns turned back to Marshal Greene. "Who is he?"

"Don't know yet," Greene said.

"I know who he is," Aaron said.

Greene's head snapped around as he looked at Aaron. "Who?"

"I saw him at the Coltrane road ranch," Aaron said. "His name is Wally."

"The idiot boy?" Burns asked.

"Yes," Aaron said. He thought but did not say aloud, *The illegitimate son of Wallace Armbrister.*

"So the Coltranes have taken to killing their own," Greene said. "But here? I can't figure it."

Burns asked Aaron, "What do you make of it?"

"Maybe they were in hiding here," Aaron said.

"Impossible," Greene said. "I've had this mansion patrolled. . . ." His voice trailed off. "I'll have the place searched, from top to bottom." He turned and walked out of the drawing room.

Aaron looked around. More damage had been done to the walls of this room. Over the fireplace he noticed that the portrait of Wallace Armbrister was gone. Then as he looked down he realized what the debris was that lay around the corpse of Wally. Someone had chopped the painting to pieces.

"What do you think, Mills?" Marshal Burns asked.

"Sadie Anne would never leave her brother's side," Aaron said. "Not voluntarily."

"You still think she's innocent?" Burns asked.

Aaron nodded. "If she's alive."

The mansion was searched from cellar to roof, but no sign of the Coltranes was found. The journalists were let into the drawing room, but did not stay long. News of another Coltrane murder sent them scurrying back to their offices. Their haste predicted the minor panic that gripped Denver the next day. Where would the Coltranes strike next? Denverites asked. Doors of residences were locked. Children were kept indoors. The section of town around Armbrister Hill was patrolled by mounted policemen. Rumors spun through Denver like dust devils. As one was discounted, another took its place.

Mae brought one rumor to Aaron two days later. Her father had heard that vigilantes had caught up with the Coltranes and lynched them.

"There is ten thousand dollars in it for the man who brings in Luke Coltrane," Aaron said. "I doubt if anybody would waste rope on him."

Mae moved closer to him. "I have a rumor that is just between the two of us: Coltrane might be coming after you, Aaron. Everyone in the West is on the lookout for him, and you're to blame."

Aaron shook his head. "Coltrane is long gone." But the words sounded hollow. Perhaps the lives of Luke Coltrane and Wallace Armbrister were intertwined in more ways than Aaron knew.

Mae interrupted his thoughts. "There's something I want you to do—for me."

"What?" Aaron asked.

"Start wearing that gun I loaned you," Mae said.

Aaron began to say no, but saw a look on her face that changed his mind. "All right, if you'll do something for me."

"What?" she asked.

"Have dinner with me tonight," Aaron said.

"That's a delicious bribe," she said, smiling. "I accept."

After the dinner date that night Aaron returned to his boarding house. Mae's suggestion that Coltrane might come looking for him had given him a case of the jitters. He drew out the small revolver from the shoulder holster and moved cautiously into the building. No one was in sight. Aaron went into his room and lit a lamp. He felt foolish as he looked around and found everything as he had left it this morning—bed unmade, clothes strewn across the floor where he had tossed them. A stranger might think the room had been ransacked. Aaron knew better.

Aaron slept little that night. The seed Mae had planted grew in the darkness to a tangle of doubts and fears, rooted in memories.

At dawn Aaron got up, feeling restless. The fact that Coltrane had been in Denver recently gave Aaron a new idea. He decided to follow some advice given to him a long time ago by the boxing coach at Hawkins Academy: when in doubt, attack.

Aaron rode his Green Machine to the *Journal* just as the sun was coming up. He worked in his office for two hours and brought the society page up to date. When Homer Witt came in, Aaron asked for the rest of the day off and got it without explaining what he intended to do.

Aaron rode his Green Machine to the City Livery, where he rented a saddle horse. He rode west out of Denver to the foothills and into the mountains through Clear Creek Canyon. He turned off at Sunrise Gulch and rode to Ross Hogan's cabin.

Aaron found the old lawman cutting wood from a dead spruce tree that had been dragged to the front of the cabin. He greeted Aaron by saying, "I wondered when you was going to get around to coming up here. I've been reading about you in the papers and wondering how much of it was true."

Aaron had nearly forgotten his promise to return here if he dug up any new evidence in the Armbrister case. "Things have been moving pretty fast for me," Aaron said.

"I heard you was hurt," Hogan said. "How you feeling now?"

"I'm all right," Aaron said, swinging down from the saddle. "My head's healing up."

Hogan laid his double-bitted axe against the tree. "Well, tell me how you busted the case open, Mills."

Aaron gave Hogan a full account of the events that led to the grisly discovery in the plowed field behind the Coltrane road ranch. Hogan listened carefully as Aaron told him that he now knew Sadie Anne and Wally were the illegitimate children of Wallace Armbrister.

"That never got in the papers," Hogan said.

"I can't prove it," Aaron said, "so I've never written it."

"But you're sure in your own mind," Hogan said.

Aaron nodded. "Sadie Anne as much as told me."

"There's a fair piece of this story that's never been put to print," Hogan observed.

"That's right," Aaron said. He went on to tell him of what he had seen in the Armbrister mansion when he had gone in with Marshal Burns and Marshal Greene.

"How do you put it all together?" Ross Hogan asked.

"I'm not sure yet," Aaron said, "but I want to look around the old Armbrister Mine. Tell me again how to get there from here."

Hogan pointed back the way Aaron had come. "Go back to Clear Creek and follow the road on up the canyon four, five miles. Armbrister Gulch comes into the canyon damn near like this one does. You'll see a big old mill at the mouth of the gulch. The mine is only a mile or so on up that gulch."

"Thanks," Aaron said. "How's your mine?"

"Oh, we're into good ground," Hogan said automatically. He paused and added, "We ain't cut the vein yet, though."

"Good luck," Aaron said. He caught his horse and mounted.

Ross Hogan grinned toothlessly. "Thanks for coming by and giving me the straight story on that Armbrister case."

Aaron turned the horse and had ridden away a short distance when Hogan called after him, "What do you aim to find up at the Armbrister mine?"

Aaron turned in the saddle and answered with a shrug, then rode into the aspen grove.

Aaron followed the road down Sunrise Gulch to Clear Creek Canyon. He rode along the canyon ore wagon road toward Armbrister Gulch. On the mountainsides he saw hundreds of prospect holes and along the creek he saw the remains of many sluice boxes. The gold mining in this region now centered around the larger mines, discoveries that had been made by the lucky few.

About two miles up the canyon Aaron saw an abandoned mill site at the mouth of a small gulch. The old mill was a long building with dark rectangles where windows had once been, and a door swung slowly on its hinges. A weathered sign over the door read ARMBRISTER MILL.

Aaron crossed Clear Creek and rode past the mill building and entered the gulch that he judged to be Armbrister Gulch. Small pine trees grew in the road.

No ore wagons had rumbled down this gulch in many years, Aaron thought.

Ahead Aaron saw a large mine dump, a heap of rust-colored earth that had been brought out of the mine. Rusting mining equipment was on top of the dump, and a pair of rails for ore cars ran into the timbered tunnel.

A strange sensation crept over Aaron, as though ghosts of the past lurked here. He grew cautious. He turned the saddle horse off the old road and rode into the thick pine forest on the opposite slope. Aaron rode along the mountainside until he was in a position where he could look across the gulch at the Armbrister Mine.

Aaron sat his horse for several minutes. He saw nothing. No signs of life but birds and squirrels and scampering chipmunks. Aaron began to feel foolish for having such a strong feeling of apprehension a few minutes ago. Then he heard a horse whinny. His saddle horse answered.

Aaron's pulse raced as he slowly rode ahead, toward the sound of the horse's call. In a break in the forest Aaron was able to see down to the bottom of the gulch. He saw a crude corral that had been built along the edge of the stream that ran there. In the corral were half a dozen horses, all looking up in Aaron's direction. One of the horses was the gelding Aaron had rented with the buggy he had driven to the Coltrane road ranch.

Aaron heard a twig snap behind him, but before he could turn, a man said, "Freeze, young 'un."

Aaron did so, but fought to control the fear that surged through him.

"Climb down off that horse," the man said.

For an agonizing moment Aaron was too frightened to move.

"I ain't going to tell you again. Climb down or I'll blow you out of the saddle."

Aaron came to life and dismounted, turning far enough as he swung down to see white-haired Luke Coltrane standing at the edge of the pine trees, aiming a double-barreled shotgun at him.

Coltrane came into the open, eyeing Aaron carefully. With one hand Coltrane reached out and slapped the horse across the rump. The saddle horse ran downslope to the stream near the corral.

"I seen you coming, young 'un," Coltrane said, moving around in front of Aaron. "You sure got a way of finding folks, don't you?"

"I'm looking for Sadie Anne," Aaron said. "Where is she?"

Coltrane's eyes flickered. "Dead."

Aaron felt nearly overcome with rage and sorrow, and for an instant he wanted to lunge at Coltrane.

"She died in Denver years ago," Coltrane said, "died after Armbrister ruined her."

Aaron took a deep breath. "I mean her daughter. Where is she?"

"Little Sadie?" Coltrane asked. "She's going to die, too. Everybody's got to die, young 'un. Even you. That's the Lord's way." He paused. "Oh, I know all about you. I starved little Sadie into telling me where you came from and how you knew her at the mansion. Yeah, I know all about you. God knows, too. I told Him. And God has spoken to me."

"Where is Sadie Anne?" Aaron asked again. "Take me to her."

"Little Sadie and Wally set you loose," Coltrane

said, seeming not to hear Aaron. "The Lord took Wally when we snuck into the mansion. I reckon you know that."

Aaron nodded.

"And that's why you came here, looking for me," Coltrane said.

"No," Aaron said, trying to hold his voice steady as he saw Coltrane's gnarled finger tighten on the trigger of the shotgun. "I'm looking for Sadie Anne."

Coltrane sneered. "The way Armbrister came looking for my Sadie Anne. Isn't that true, young 'un? You aim to use her like Armbrister used my girl. Ruined her, he did." He paused. "You think you know all about me, but you don't. You don't know nothing. Me and the Lord knows."

Aaron hoped to keep the old man talking. "Know what?"

"About the Armbristers and why all those men had to die," Coltrane said.

"Tell me," Aaron said, "so I'll understand."

"The Lord provides," Coltrane said. "The Lord brought those men to me over the years. He provides. Kept me from starving out, He did. But now the whole damned country's hunting me. Lynch mobs is after me. Trying to crucify me. All because of you. But now the good Lord is fixing to make you pay."

Aaron said, "Take me to her. Take me to Sadie Anne."

Coltrane smiled, then nodded once. He motioned with the barrel of the shotgun. "Go on over to the mine."

Aaron walked ahead of Luke Coltrane down the slope toward the creek. He put his right hand over his chest and quickly worked a coat button loose. He slid his hand into the opening just as Coltrane punched him hard in the back with the barrel of the shotgun.

"Keep your hands out where I can see them."

Aaron hesitated, then held his hands out. He waded the stream and heard Coltrane splash through behind him. He climbed to the top of the mine dump, and as he approached the dark mouth of the tunnel, Coltrane ordered him to stop.

"Pull off your boots."

Aaron took them off as Coltrane watched.

"Now your belt."

Aaron unhooked his belt and slid it out of his trouser belt loops.

"Turn around," Coltrane said. "Put your hands behind you."

Aaron heard Coltrane move close behind him, then he felt the leather belt circle his wrists. As the belt tightened, Aaron realized he had missed his chance to go for the revolver in the shoulder holster. He had been indecisive, and now it was too late.

Coltrane went to the tunnel and picked up a lantern. He set the shotgun down for a moment while he lit the lantern. Then he picked both up, placing the lantern's wire handle over the barrel of the shotgun. He pointed the shotgun at Aaron's chest.

"Go on in," Coltrane said, jerking his head toward the mine tunnel.

Aaron walked gingerly into the dark, cool mouth of the mine. Wavering light came behind him as Coltrane followed. Aaron quickly found that by walking along the narrowly spaced ties between the rails, he saved his feet from injury on the sharp rocks. As

Aaron walked, he struggled against the belt around his wrists by slowly turning one hand and pulling while pushing down with the other hand.

"You ain't going to bust loose," Coltrane said. "Quit your damned fighting."

Deep in the Armbrister Mine they entered an underground room. By the light of Coltrane's lantern, Aaron saw two other tunnels branching off from the main one. In the middle of the underground room an ore car sat on the rails. Around it was a pile of gear, canned food, and blankets. Off to his right Aaron heard a moan.

By the uncertain light of the lantern, Aaron saw the figure of a woman slumped against the timbered wall of the mine.

"Sadie Anne!" Aaron said.

Chapter XVIII

Aaron rushed to her, stumbling over an unseen pile of rocks. Pain shot through his feet as he regained his balance. He dropped to his knees beside Sadie Anne. She moaned again, blinking slowly.

"Sadie Anne," Aaron said again.

Her cracked lips moved. She turned her head toward Aaron.

"Here," Coltrane said, coming up behind them. Coltrane held a canteen high over her upturned face and let water dribble down.

Sadie Anne licked her lips as the water struck her face and ran to her mouth. She raised one hand, reaching for the canteen.

Coltrane laughed. "That's enough, little Sadie."

Aaron looked up at Coltrane. "Free my hands so I can help her."

Coltrane replied by kicking him in the ribs. "Move away from little Sadie. Go on." He kicked Aaron again.

Aaron edged away a short distance. He turned and sat down, leaning back against the cold rock wall. He worked frantically to pull his wrists out of the tightly knotted belt.

Coltrane walked back to the ore car in the center of the underground room. He set the shotgun on top of the ore car, but he watched Aaron suspiciously. Then, apparently as an afterthought, he came back to Aaron.

Coltrane stooped down, noticing that one of Aaron's coat buttons was undone. He unbuttoned the other buttons. Coltrane lifted the coat open by the lapels.

"Well, look here," Coltrane said, taking the small revolver from the shoulder holster. "A sneak gun. No wonder you've been fighting to get your hands loose."

Coltrane stood. He held the revolver to the light that came from the lantern on the ore car. "I haven't seen one of these since I put a bullet through Wallace Armbrister's head."

For a moment Aaron was too surprised to speak. "You . . . you shot Wallace Armbrister?"

Coltrane nodded.

"Why?" Aaron asked.

Coltrane looked down at Aaron. "I reckon it don't matter if you know. My Sadie Anne ran off to Denver years ago. I thought I'd lost her forever, but then she wrote to me and said she'd had two children by Wallace Armbrister and Armbrister had threatened to kill them. She wanted to get away from Armbrister, but she knew he would track her down. She was afraid to come home."

Aaron asked, "Why would Armbrister want to kill his own children?"

"You seen Wally," Coltrane said. "Armbrister feared madness was in his family. Wallace Armbrister was an agent of the devil. I left my road ranch and went to the Western Hotel. I pleaded with Sadie Anne to come home with me, but she was too afraid of Armbrister to leave. Then Armbrister came to her room. I rassled him down and took his sneak gun and shot him through the head with it. I done the Lord's good work, young 'un. I rassled the devil and whupped him."

For a moment Coltrane's eyes brightened as he relived the triumph. "Sadie Anne sneaked me out of her room before anyone came. She promised to come home, but she never did. The next thing I knowed, folks was saying Wallace Armbrister killed himself. I reckon Sadie Anne stuck with that story, and some of her friends backed her up." He paused. "But then Sadie Anne died the next year, and I went and got her children."

The silence that followed was broken by the raspy voice of Sadie Anne. "You murdered Wally."

"God willed it, little Sadie," Coltrane said. "Wally's in God's heaven now, resting in peace."

Sadie Anne turned to Aaron. "He sold me to Mrs. Armbrister, Aaron."

Coltrane laughed suddenly. "You was willing." To Aaron he said, "I went to the old lady's mansion after I got the children. I told Mrs. Armbrister she would have to pay, but she ran me off her property. Then a few years later she came to me. She wanted little Sadie."

Sadie Anne said, "She promised to take in Wally, too, if I learned to become a proper lady. But she broke her promise."

"And she never paid me enough," Coltrane said. "I went back for more. She owed me. And the good Lord made her pay." Coltrane had been holding the small revolver in his hand, but now he dropped it into his coat pocket. He looked at Aaron.

"I have done God's work," Coltrane said. "I weed out the weak and the worthless." He bent down beside the ore car and picked up an axe. He came toward Aaron. "I know about you and little Sadie. You came after her the way the devil comes for the sinful." He raised the axe.

"No!" Sadie Anne screamed.

Aaron struggled against the belt that bound his wrists. At the same time he tried to scramble to his feet. Coltrane approached slowly, mumbling in a low voice.

"I shall do God's work, I shall do God's work."

Sadie Anne shrieked again.

"Coltrane!" The sudden, commanding voice came from the other end of the underground room.

Coltrane stopped, then slowly turned around.

"Let that axe drop. Real easy now."

Aaron could not see the man, but he recognized the voice of Ross Hogan. The old lawman stepped farther into the underground room, aiming his revolver at Coltrane.

The axe slipped from Coltrane's hands, clattering against the rocks at his feet. Hogan looked past him at Aaron.

"Are you all right?"

"Yes," Aaron said, but he noticed Coltrane's hand dart into his coat pocket. Aaron realized what was happening, but for an agonizing instant he was paralyzed. Then Aaron shouted, "Gun! He has a gun!"

Coltrane moved quickly. He drew the small pistol out of his pocket and swung around, taking aim at Hogan. Hogan leveled his revolver at Coltrane's chest and pulled the trigger.

The roar in the underground room was deafening. Coltrane was slammed against the wall of the mine, a look of disbelief on his face. He kept his feet for a moment, appearing to stare at Hogan, then he gasped and fell forward. Coltrane lay still on the rocky floor of the mine.

Powder smoke was thick in the air. The long silence that followed the shooting was finally broken by Hogan. "Hell, I didn't want to kill him."

Aaron struggled to his feet. Hogan freed his hands. Aaron knelt beside Sadie Anne and then helped her stand. She was very weak.

"I haven't eaten since . . ." She nearly fainted. Aaron caught her and took her in his arms. He carried her out of the mine, walking carefully on the ties. Outside he set Sadie Anne down and then put on his boots. He returned to the underground room and helped Hogan carry out the body of Luke Coltrane.

"I'm glad you came," Aaron said to Hogan, "but I don't know why you did."

"After you left I got to thinking that you must have been on to something," Hogan said. "I wondered exactly what you aimed to find here. Then I got an idea that this might be a hiding place for the Coltranes. I saddled my horse and rode up here. I found that remuda down by the crick. Up on the mine dump I found a pair of boots. Then I heard the girl holler." He added, "Mills, you shouldn't have come here alone."

"I had a hunch Coltrane might be here," Aaron said, "but I never really expected to find him."

"Well, you found him," Hogan said. He grinned. "I reckon we ought to split the reward."

"No," Aaron said, "the reward is yours. You earned it. I won't take a penny of that money."

They set the body of Luke Coltrane down outside the mouth of the tunnel. The fresh air and sunlight revived Sadie Anne. With Aaron's help, she stood.

Hogan looked into the dark mine entrance. "I figured I'd make a fortune in a mine, but I never guessed I'd do it this way."

Chapter XIX

The shooting of Luke Coltrane caused a nationwide sensation. And once again, Aaron's front page story in the *Denver City Journal* became the basis of all the published accounts.

Ross Hogan became a local hero. Denver's mayor proclaimed a "Ross Hogan Day." After the body of Luke Coltrane was officially identified, Hogan collected his $10,000 reward in a ceremony at the state capitol building.

At the close of the ceremony, Ross Hogan said privately to Aaron and Mae Catton, "I never got this kind of treatment when I retired."

Sadie Anne was arrested and charged as an accomplice to a murderer. She was placed under the care of a doctor after her severe case of malnutrition was diagnosed. Aaron visited her several times while she was in custody. The meetings were uncomfortable to Aaron, but he tried to cheer Sadie Anne. She told Aaron that she expected to be convicted and hanged.

"No, you won't," Aaron said. "You're not guilty of being an accomplice to a murderer."

"How do you know?" she asked.

"Sadie Anne," Aaron said, taking her hand, "I believe in you."

For once, she smiled.

The trial was held in a Denver courtroom three weeks later. Homer Witt assigned Aaron to cover the trial, over the strong objections of Henry Daniels. Daniels threatened to resign, and Witt threatened to accept his resignation.

Mae attended much of the trial with Aaron. The proceedings lasted four days. For two hours one morning Aaron testified about what he knew of Sadie Anne. He described how she had saved his life when she freed him from the cellar at the Coltrane road ranch.

Sadie Anne testified in her own defense, giving evidence that she was Luke Coltrane's prisoner from the time she learned of the murders in the Armbrister mansion to the time of Coltrane's death in the Armbrister mine. She told of her attempts to escape from the road ranch. The attempts had always been foiled by Wally, who returned to the only home he had ever known. The escape attempts ended when Luke Coltrane told Sadie Anne he would kill Wally the next time she tried to run away.

Sadie Anne also testified that she had never actually witnessed a murder. She learned of the murders in the Armbrister mansion only after they were known to the public. That marked her first attempt to escape from Luke Coltrane.

When a traveler came to the road ranch, Sadie Anne testified, she took her brother to the far end of the sod house. She knew they lived with a madman and she thought they might be killed by him one day.

The jury deliberated for less than half a day. They returned a verdict of innocent.

All the journalists but Aaron rushed out of the courtroom to file their stories. Aaron remained seated until all the spectators had gone. Aaron watched

Sadie Anne say good-by to her attorney. When she turned toward the aisle, she saw Aaron. She came to him.

They looked into one another's eyes for several moments. A certain communication passed between them. Sadie Anne was Aaron's first love, but not his last.

"I'm going away," she said.

"Where?" Aaron asked.

She shrugged. "Far away. I'll make a new start."

Aaron nodded.

Sadie Anne moved close to him. "You believed in me, Aaron."

Aaron put his arms around her and held her tightly. "I still do."

After the embrace, they parted without saying good-by. Aaron watched her walk out of the courtroom. He stayed there a few minutes, alone with his thoughts and memories. Then he left and returned to his office.

Aaron wrote the final article in his account of the trial. He put his pen down and thought back over the last ten years of his life. He was aware of a particular moment when he had left his boyhood behind. The memory was a poignant one, but no longer painful.

Aaron thought back to an observation Mae had made when they'd slept out under the stars. "Everybody changes, Aaron, all the time." Aaron thought back over the last ten years. Now he saw meaning and direction in seemingly unrelated events, and he realized he had changed and he had grown. Aaron wondered if he would change as much in the next ten years, and if he would be faced by as many challenges.

Homer Witt tapped on Aaron's office door and came in. "How's the article coming?"

"It's finished," Aaron said.

"Good," Witt said. He sat on the corner of Aaron's desk. "Daniels is gone."

"Gone?" Aaron said in surprise.

Witt's eyebrows bobbed rapidly. "He quit today. I understand he's been trying to get on with the *Rocky Mountain News* for some time. Now he's over there."

Witt paused. "I called Sam Catton into my office a while ago. We had a long talk. He admitted that Daniels had tried to talk him into resigning and going over to the *News*. I had suspected as much, so it was no surprise. Sam's staying on, though." Witt added, "He's been off the bottle for quite a while now, you know."

"So I've heard," Aaron said.

"I've always believed Sam is a good man," Witt said. "And he has a lot of savvy about newspapers. I offered him the job of city editor."

"Did he accept?" Aaron asked.

"He did," Witt said. "I thought he might not take to the idea of being tied down to a desk all day, but Sam said he was ready for a desk job. I believe he is, too. He's been on the streets most of his life." Witt paused. "We agreed on a successor to his position—you."

Aaron was surprised at the offer, but he said, "Sam agreed to that?"

"Yes," Witt said. "You might be amazed at the way he talks about you behind your back."

Aaron laughed. "Maybe I would."

"Will you take the job of crime writer for the *Journal*?" Witt asked.

"I'll take it," Aaron said. He stood and shook hands with Homer Witt.

"What's Mae going to think about all this?" Witt asked, eyebrows bobbing.

"I don't know," Aaron said. He was anxious to find out.

Stephen Overholser was born in Bend, Oregon, the middle son of Western author, Wayne D. Overholser. Convinced, in his words, that "there was more to learn outside of school than inside," he left Colorado State College in his senior year. He was drafted and served in the U.S. Army in Vietnam. Following his discharge, he launched his career as a writer, publishing three short stories in *Zane Grey Western Magazine*. On a research visit to the University of Wyoming at Laramie, he came across an account of a shocking incident that preceded the Johnson County War in Wyoming in 1892. It was this incident that became the inspiration for his first novel, *A Hanging at Sweetwater* (1974), that received the Spur Award from the Western Writers of America. *Molly and the Confidence Man* (1975) followed, the first in a series of books about Molly Owens, a clever, resourceful, and tough undercover operative working for a fictional detective agency in the Old West. Among the most notable of Stephen Overholser's later titles are *Search for the Fox* (1976) and *Track of a Killer* (1982). Stephen Overholser's latest novel is *Dark Embers at Dawn*.